claimed

EDGE book 1

JENNA HOWARD

For the bestie who asked why she had no dedication. I didn't have an answer aside from the fact that there were no books. Now there is. So here you go Cassie…your dedication.

I'd also like to thank Sasha White (again) because really…this was a long time coming and thanks to you asking about Yield…along came Claimed…finally.

Dear Reader,

When I wrote Yield in 2015, there had been the plan had been to write a series but then the characters I had picked had gone quiet and nothing I did woke them up. I had even contemplated the idea of a prequel with Oz and Claire because hello…Doyle's best friend and ex-wife? Yaaaaas. But again…I couldn't figure out how their story came together.

Flash forward to 2018 and it's the day after Calgary's first romance reader festival, Sultry & Sweet Summer Reads YYC. I hung with writers. More…I talked about Yield to Sasha White (ooooh man…I talked to SASHA freakin' WHITE!) and I realized I loved that story. I loved the characters, I loved their relationship with each other and others around them.

There's nothing like a little nudge to get awaken the brain and so here I am…traveling to 2008/2009 when Oz and Claire took things to another level. The series may be out written out of order but this is very much book 1. This is before Kate, before Yield. This…is Oz and Claire.

Finally.

Oz and Claire also play on the naughty side where it's all safe, sane and consensual.

Chapter 1

December 30, 2008

NOTHING RUINED A blowjob like hearing the words: "Boss, you're needed in the pit."

Tucking his dick back into his pants, Oz Peters uncuffed the submissive from his chair and left her kneeling with her head resting on the floor, the vibrator silent but still buried within her. He hadn't opened the window that separated his office from the club, giving them the illusion of privacy. He trusted his dungeon monitors to keep the club going for an hour or two while he did some paperwork, with an eager mouth wrapped around his dick to properly motivate him to finish. That his crew called for him told him that whatever was happening in the club was serious shit.

Two of his DMs were standing at one of the entrances to the pit, arms folded and eyebrows furrowed. He followed those frustrated stares to a scene going off the rails. One look was all it took. The submissive was not just tied to a spanking bench but cuffed and her body was covered in red welts. "You didn't stop him?"

"*She*," Davis growled, "wouldn't let us."

Oz gave his employees a hard look because they had one job: to keep everyone safe. He didn't give a damn what they did to protect all of the members, even those too stupid to stop, be they dominant or submissive. All other scenes were gradually coming to a stop, because nothing killed the mood like a scene going downhill.

"Sorry, Oz," Jasmine, one of the dommes, said quietly to him as he passed. "She is…I can't…I tried."

It wasn't Jasmine's job to stop a scene. She had one job and that was to have a good time with her sub. Walking by, he grabbed the dom's forearm when he went to deliver another blow of a heavy strap to the sub's painfully bruised body. Jesus Christ. "You are done," he said in a low voice.

"She said…"

"I say you are done."

"No," she screamed, writhing. There was a lot of pain and anger in that one word. He swore he heard her tears falling to the padded floor. She could scream at him all she wanted. This shit was fucking done.

"This," he yanked the strap from the man's hand and flung it aside – the heavy leather making a loud thud in the quiet club, "does not happen here. Get your shit and get out. I will see you here tomorrow and we'll discuss whether I refund you every fucking dollar or you save your ass from getting kicked out. Davis!" Davis jerked at his named barked at him. "Do your fucking job. Everyone. Wrap it up. Pit is closed. You have an hour for aftercare but we are fucking done. You." He pointed at a sub who was standing at the edge of the pit, watching, her face pale and her hands gripping the railing. He knew her name but right now he couldn't untangle it. "Have you played tonight?"

"No, Sir."

"Joanie is in my office. If you could remove everything and stay with her, I would greatly appreciate it." She nodded and ran around the curved room, bolting into his office. "Now. You."

The sub was sobbing. Her bound body jerked with every wrenched sound from her. Fuck. Exhaling twice to push out the anger, he walked to where her head hung down. He snapped his fingers at one of his employees and they hurried over, drawing safety shears from their pocket to cut the ropes free. Squatting down, he slid his hand under the woman's face and tilted her head up.

Well.

"Fuck."

Her face was red, her lips swollen and bloody where she had bit down. Her eyes were swollen from tears that still fell. Her auburn hair hung limply over a face dripping with failure. "I need this, Oz."

"Oh, Claire," he whispered as he wiped his thumb over one soaked cheek. It had been over two years since Claire Kolemann had been in his club. When her marriage to his best friend had fallen apart, Claire had decided to not return. She probably did need something, but as far as he was concerned, she wasn't a masochist. Pain wasn't what made this submissive hum.

Certainly not this kind of pain.

Anyone who needed this kind of pain knew to come to him and he'd arrange for a private night with the sadists and masochists because what covered Claire's back wasn't everyone's cup of kink.

A nod from his guy said she was clear of any and all bindings though she still hugged the bench like she was bound.

The pit was empty and it felt wrong because the club wasn't empty. There was a solemn tinge to the air, making everything feel off. Gently, he lowered her head and straightened, eyeing her poor body. He had no idea how to get her off the bench without causing her significant pain. He was all about discomfort in his submissives, but this was not what he looked for either of them to get off.

He didn't know what had driven Claire to Edge tonight. What had pushed her to punish her body so hard that looking at her hurt?

Fuck. This was going to suck ass. "Hold her under her thighs here and we'll get her upright. Do not let that ass rest on the leather."

"Got it."

He moved to her head and sank down once more. "I'm not going to lie, sweetheart, this is going to hurt. I'll be honest, I'm fighting the urge to toss you in my car and drive you to Emergency because damn, baby, you are a fucking mess."

"No. Oz. No! Doyle can't know."

He snorted. Doyle would figure it out when he saw the condition of his ex-wife's body. Jesus, he wished his friend was on tour, because when he saw Claire, he was going to kick Oz's ass. Doyle was a big motherfucker with heavily muscled arms so he could bang the hell out of the drums for the rock band Cyanide. The man could hit.

Oz had no desire to be hit.

With a little help, he got Claire upright. A pained cry

and sucked-in breath came from her. Her flushed face went white and terrified blue eyes looked at him. That's right, sweetheart, he thought as he lifted her up like she was a child, you fucking destroyed your body.

There was no safe place to put his hands so he cupped her thighs to hold her. Teeth sank into his shoulder and he grunted at the bite. Eyes watched him carry her off out of the pit and into his office. Joanie and Jessica, the sub he had sent to his office, took one look at Claire. They turned tear-filled eyes at him.

"Jessica, can you get me some water?"

"Yes, Sir."

Joanie pointed at herself, gave him a thumbs-up, and followed the other submissive out, shutting the door.

Usually when he shut Edge down early, he stayed to supervise. The BDSM club was his pride and joy. His kingdom may be small and kinky, but he was well aware of his responsibility within these walls. Right now, that was the woman he held. "This isn't going to be fun, Claire," he warned as he sank down onto the couch, turned and slowly lay down so she was sprawled on his chest. He hissed as her bite went a bit harder. "Teeth, Claire."

When there was no response he fisted his hand in her hair, tugged without pulling because her teeth were currently in his shoulder. Fuck the kindness. "Let loose. Now." He snapped the words out like he would to a bratty sub. The response was instantaneous. Her jaw relaxed, releasing him. He eased his grip on her hair, nudging her head down so her cheek rested where she had been chomping on him.

"You can't tell Doyle, Oz."

"Do you think he won't notice you won't be able to

move or you'll whimper the minute you pick up one of the girls? How do you see this going, Claire? Have you seen your back?"

"You can't tell him. Promise."

"No."

She sat up to glare at him and her eyes went large and the freckles on her face stood out in stark contrast to how white she went.

"If you can walk into the bathroom, I can show you exactly what you made him do. You want to tell me what that was about?"

"No."

"Let me rephrase that." He grabbed her chin and made her look at him. "You will tell me what that was about."

A mutinous look came across her face, like when one of her girls was misbehaving, knew it but wasn't about to cop to it. "You're not my dom, Oscar Peters."

"You're right, Claire Kolemann." Fed up, he sat up and pushed her off. She sucked in her breath and hopped to her feet, her hand hovering over her ass. "There's a vast difference between me topping you and being concerned about your well-being. You can write me an essay on that. In three weeks, you'll be back in this office. Four o'clock."

She got that pissy look and he bent his knees so their eyes were level. "You broke club rules. There are consequences. Just like the talk tomorrow I'll have with the dom, I'll determine your future within this club." He opened his door and shouted for Jessica. "Help her get dressed then put her in a cab. When she checks out of her hotel tomorrow, she can pick up her car. We're done here." He left his office before he did something he was pretty sure wasn't wise. He had a low tolerance for bratty subs and his corrective measures were often swift and final.

As Claire herself had said – he wasn't her dom, nothing had been negotiated; the best he could do was remove himself from a situation that was hitting his "hell fucking no" button.

She had screwed up. Beyond screwed up. Not just with Oz and the dom whose name she couldn't even remember, but with everything. Rubbing the heel of her hand over her forehead, Claire tried to figure out how to get out of this mess. Oz was right. There was no way Doyle wouldn't notice something was wrong the minute he saw her. The man was observant. Especially now that he was sober.

Hell, even if he had been high and drunk, he'd know she was messed up. Because holy crap.

No wonder Oz was pissed at her.

The back of her body looked like…she couldn't even think of an analogy for how she looked. The minute the other submissive had walked her into the women's change room, Claire had twisted at the full-length mirror by the door to see how bad everything was. She wasn't a masochist. Pain wasn't what got her off so what the hell had happened tonight?

She knew. But holy crap…what was she doing?

One particularly wide slash over the top of her shoulders made tears burn when she reached up to prod it. Her stomach gave another nervous twist, as she turned to face herself. She wore her whitest, laciest thong. Before her scene, she had been wearing a navy and grey plaid skirt that had ended just at the lowest curve of her ass, a white cropped blouse tied beneath her breasts and over the knee white socks. A tie matched her skirt and with two ponytails in her hair, she had looked like a naughty school girl. Now, however, she looked like that naughty school girl had been flattened by life a few times.

Until she had pulled the outfit out of storage, she had made herself forget how much she loved dressing up in costumes. Doyle had happily indulged her with a fortune in fetish wear and cosplay outfits. When her marriage began to fall apart, they stopped scening. The old-fashioned trunks went into storage because knowing they were around had hurt her heart.

When she unlocked the first trunk, she hadn't realized how deeply she had buried her love of them. In the middle of the storage locker, she sat on the concrete floor and wept for the woman who loved being surprised by her husband, and her dom treating her to something she loved. She cried over the fact that he wasn't going to see her in her choice, work her over then spend the rest of the night fucking them both into oblivion.

Now look at her.

She had no idea where her costume was, no idea who she had scened with, if one could call whatever tonight had been a scene, and her body was a mess. The thought of opening the locker she had been assigned for the night and putting on her clothes exhausted her. Exactly how was she going to get her jeans on? And her top? What about her shoes?

Once again, she twisted to look over her shoulder, staring at the marks.

Reaching down, she lightly brushed her fingers over

a red welt at the crease where thigh met ass. She was sure it had been one of the early strokes because she could still recall the powerful strike that also hit her pussy. It had hurt, a lot. But it had been a familiar pain, one that curled through her body, pulsing in time to her heart beat and send pain endorphins to the sensitive area. The orgasm had been welcome and yet unwelcome because the spot was her ex's favorite location to spank, especially when he wanted to make her come without granting her permission. She couldn't remember the last time she came from a blow there. Or had an orgasm, period.

Was that the moment she lost it? Because some anonymous, already forgotten man hadn't just aroused her but made her come? Or had she lost it before then?

"Are you admiring or loathing the marks?"

She jumped at the voice and spun to see the door open and Oz watching her fondle her ass. She shrugged, unsure of the answer. He studied her, his face expressionless although she suddenly became aware she was naked but for her panties. Tension rippled through her as he stepped into the women's locker room, letting the door quietly shut. In one hand was her missing outfit.

"Let's get you dressed as you think over the answer."

She felt incredibly vulnerable as she unlocked the combination lock she brought. Oz opened the locker door, and pulled her clothes out. He was quiet as he dropped down into a squat, one of her socks in his hand.

Gripping the edge of the locker, she lifted a foot, watching as he slid her socks into place. Next he reached for her jeans and she dreaded this part. She had clearly forgotten a few things in the past few years because she had gone for style over comfort. The skinny jeans that she had been proud to wiggle into were now her idea of hell and she wasn't even wearing them yet.

Exhaling slowly, she lifted one foot and watched as Oz slid the denim around her ankle then the other leg. She couldn't remember the last time anyone had dressed her. Doyle used to with her fetish wear, but that had been part of the seduction. This was something else entirely different.

Oz guided the jeans up and she winced as the fabric brushed over highly sensitive skin. Short dark blond strands of hair tickled her stomach as he eased her jeans up her thighs, one hand tucked between the fabric and her heavily marked thighs. His palm was surprisingly gentle as it formed a barricade and the dual sensations caught her by surprise. The care wasn't sensual at all, but her body didn't recognize that. As she looked down at him, she watched in mortification as her nipples swelled into needy points and both her ass and stomach tightened while that narrow swatch of lace between her legs grew damp.

Oz cupped her hips and turned her so she faced the lockers and not him. Her eyes closed as his hands lightly stroked over her ass, down her thighs to where her jeans waited. She tried to tell herself that this was her ex-husband's best friend, her ex-dom's best friend, but her body didn't give a shit. Her hands slammed into the locker door beside hers when thumbs traced that one mark beneath her ass. There was enough pressure to make the tender nerves sing awake and she felt her pussy soften at the slight pain beneath the touch. From hip to the inside of her thighs, he rubbed back and forth until her panties weren't just damp but soaked, her body well aware that a master knew just how to touch.

Her breathing grew shaky as her ass tilted up. Soft pants escaped as he tugged the sides of her thong down. He squeezed her abused ass with strong hands that made her cry out, and not in pain. His fingers moved and found every tender spot and he pressed gently, manipulating the pain into hot, pulsing pleasure. She was so wet and she knew he could see it where he knelt and that made her wetter, made her body writhe as he worked her pain points.

Warm hands glided up her sides and slid around to cup her breasts, pinching and pulling on her nipples as he pressed his erection against her throbbing ass.

"I'm going to make you come, Claire."

Oh. God. *Yes.*

"With my hands and with my paddle." His voice was low and soothing against her ear. His hands squeezed her breasts with enough force to make her cry out and push her ass into that thick cock trapped behind fabric. "I'm going to make you scream. Make you beg. Make you come. I'm going to put you on that bench again and show you how good the pain can be."

She was going to come as she rubbed against him, his fingers still seeking and finding places that made her cry out, made her pussy slick and made her body hum in a delightful way. "When you're slick and swollen from all your cum, I'm going to fill your pussy and fuck you until you beg me for my cum."

Her hips twisted and she ground against his cock, so hard against where she was so wet. Cries of pain and pleasure echoed in the room, her body straining for the orgasm, to feel him inside her where she ached.

He pushed his hips forward, nudging her aching clit with his cock and her body went liquid. She was going to come. Holy crap, he was going to make her come.

"But not tonight. You haven't earned that orgasm yet. You certainly haven't earned my cum."

A hot pulse of heat pumped through her to where he rested but his hands were already guiding her hips away.

"No," she whispered.

"I don't reward brattiness with fucking," he said, the liquid sex leaving his voice so it had a bite of control in it. His hand slapped down on her ass and she cried out – this time in pain because shit…it hurt. Without any hesitation, he drew her jeans up and spun her around again so he could button and zip the fly. "Three weeks, you'll be here at four o'clock." He finished dressing her like she was a mannequin. One who was shaking and on the break of climax.

He walked her out and tucked her into a cab before she fully realized what had happened.

Oscar Peters had totally topped her in his club.

Oz – October 1989

There were times when Oscar really hated his roommates. If his situation had been different, he'd have his own room. Instead, he was sharing with three other guys he had nothing in common with. Even with his Walkman turned up high, his three roommates were loud and obnoxious enough to drown out Tchaikovsky being played on the piano.

Everyone had been assigned to the room and the minute Oz had laid eyes on them, he had known the year was going to be rough. There was Aaron Kyle, who was in business but so far all Oz had seen him do was get drunk with the fraternity he had joined. There was something smarmy about him. He talked about all the girls he had laid so far, but Oz had yet to see a girl around him. Next was Jesse Hernández, a guy from a small town in Saskatchewan who was madly in love with his girlfriend and they were constantly at it, which was a real bitch since Jesse's bed was in the same room as Oz. Jesse was in journalism and when his girlfriend was around – nice guy. When he was hanging with the guys here, utter asshole. Finally, there was Joshua Avery who, Oz was sure, was the biggest asshole ever. He was in forestry and was not just a jerk but a fucking jerk.

It wasn't the girls that cycled through the room, then came looking for Avery when he ditched them, or that he was a bully, he was just an all-round asshole. He had decided that Oz was the perfect patsy to his dick behavior.

Maybe he wasn't as muscular as Avery and the others, but he was also no pushover. He wasn't at UBC to drink himself into a vomiting idiot, he wasn't here to fuck his way through the female classmates. He had a plan. He was utterly focused on getting his degree in architecture; being a university douche wasn't listed anywhere in his plans.

"Hey asswipe, you should come hang with us tonight." Avery shouted right in his ear, because he was an asshole.

"I have things to do."

"Nerd. Seriously, you should come. I heard about this party and Kendall is bringing some friends."

Awesome. Because if Avery was an asshole, Kendall

was the queen bitch to his crown. She was the latest girl and so far, she was lasting the longest.

"I'm good."

"There's more to life than school, Peters. You should pop that cherry and get your dick wet."

"Uh-huh." For whatever reason, Avery had taken one look at him and decided he was a virgin. Because in his roommates' world, only jock types got laid. Oz hadn't bothered to correct him.

"Your loss. This party is going to be fucking awe-some." He high-fived Jesse.

Uh-huh. Oz removed his glasses, wiping them off on his shirt. "So why invite me?"

Jesse snorted into his fist and Oz was done with the conversation.

Someone knocked on the door and from Avery's swagger, it was Kendall. Sure enough, the bitchy blonde led a crew of friends into the room. She and Avery kissed and it was a nasty slathering of tongues and ass grabbing.

His gaze scanned over the girls, landing on the last one. She didn't look like she fit in with the scantily clad, teased-out hair girls. Her dark brown hair was pulled back in a braid and unlike the others, she wore a but-toned blouse and a floral skirt. She fit in with them like he did.

Narrowing his eyes, he scanned everyone before looking back at her. You didn't take a misfit along unless you were planning on being a dick. Damn it.

"On second thought–" He removed the earphones and turned off the tape, tucking the machine into his desk.

"That's what I'm talking about. Peters, meet the ladies." He slapped Kendall's ass and she flipped her permed hair over her shoulder.

"This is Ashley, Brandy, Kristin and my roommate, Olivia."

Tossing his glasses onto his desk, Oz grabbed his jacket as the swarm left the room. Aaron passed around a flask he thought was cool. Oz and Olivia were the only ones who didn't drink. Kendall razzed the quiet girl but she simply blushed and shook her head.

What was this girl doing with them? Tucking his hands into his pockets, he slowed his steps so he was beside her. "Hey, I'm Oz."

Her cheeks went bright red and she looked everywhere but at him. Cute. She smoothed her hand over her braid in a nervous move. "Hi." She had a soft sweet voice, utterly at odds with the boisterous shrieks of laughter coming from Kendall. "I'm Olivia."

He wanted to ask her how she had wound up with this group but decided that was a little rude. "I'm in architecture. You?"

"Anthropology."

"What does one do in anthropology?"

She blushed again. "Cultures intrigue me so I want to know more."

"What's your favorite?"

"You'll laugh."

Oz stopped and looked into her brown eyes. "I don't laugh at people's passions."

"But...Josh..."

"Is a dick. Tell me what made you choose anthropology." They walked behind the others and Olivia told him about her indigenous background and how her history intrigued her, especially the languages. Seriously cool.

Once he got her talking, she seemed to relax a little. Oz wasn't entirely sure how long they had been walking, but a lot of bitching about sore feet from sky high heels began to trickle from the girls. He had handed over his jacket to Olivia ten minutes ago when a little shiver had moved through her.

It wasn't that cold, but neither was it warm. At least it wasn't raining, which made for a change in Vancouver. Though that could turn on them in a minute.

"This is it!" Avery declared and Oz studied the house.

It didn't look like a party was happening. Avery and Kendall led the way across someone's lawn and up the stairs, where he pounded on the door. Jesse lit up a ciga-rette and shared it with one of the girls.

When the door opened, Oz's suspicions began to rise because no way was that guy in university. Kendall made a production out of a missing earring and she told Olivia to wait inside. Whispering she needed the bathroom, the quiet girl made for the door.

"Peters, we'll be right in. Gotta find my girl's jewelry."

Left with no real choice because he wasn't going to leave Olivia behind, Oz stepped into the house.

"Shoes off. You want a beer?"

"No." Oz toed off his sneakers and followed the guy into the house. His entire body froze as he gawked.

This was no kegger party.

Not judging by the naked woman tied to a giant X while some guy hit her with a whip.

Chapter 2

WHEN CLAIRE AND Doyle had built the house, she had envisioned them living here forever, happy in love with their beautiful babies. That hadn't happened. Instead she lived here with their beautiful daughters and her ex-husband owned the land next door and built his own home. She had been so angry when Doyle had decided to do that, until she realized how happy it made the girls. They could go over whenever they wanted, as long as one of them walked them over either way. It also meant her house was empty when she finally arrived after a sleepless night at the hotel.

She couldn't even blame the scene from the club.

Over and over, all she heard was Oz's voice: *"I'm going to make you scream. Make you beg. Make you come. I'm going to put you on that bench again and show you how good the pain can be."*

She didn't want pain. Right?

That wasn't the type of sub she was. Oh, Doyle knew how to wield his impact toys, but she had a feeling Oz was talking about a different kind of pain. To her knowledge, he wasn't a sadist, that was Doyle's other best friend from the club. She certainly wasn't a masochist, but there had been no denying what Oz had done just with his fingers and her sore body.

He had made her body hum.

Like it was now just remembering.

Thank God the house was silent. She made her way into the master bathroom. Turning the water on in the tub, Claire slowly stripped out of the clothes she had slept in, half afraid she wouldn't be able to dress in the morning. Entering her walk-in closet, she turned so her back was to the full-length mirror. Some of the redness was fading to pink but she was definitely going to have some bruising. The two ferry rides home felt like they had taken days. The motion of the boats, sore muscles, a body ricocheting between pain and arousal – it had been a very long journey home.

Her fingers ran along the mark below her ass and she remembered Oz's fingers pressing into the tender skin as he caressed back and forth.

And she was aroused again.

With a tired sigh, she left all her clothes on the floor. Throwing some epsom salts and dried lavender buds into the water, Claire stepped in and slowly, so slowly, sank down. As soon as the hot water hit tender skin, she hissed. Still, the heat soaked into tense muscles in a delicious way.

As the water settled around her, she slipped her hand between her legs. He hadn't said she couldn't come without his permission. All he had done was make a pile of promises. A pile of sexy, dirty promises.

She could easily imagine him tying her to the spanking bench, the cool leather against skin prickling with nerves and awareness. She'd be naked so he could see every response of her body, how wet she became beneath his hands and paddle and how red her skin would become beneath his blows.

Beneath the water, her hips twitched as she rubbed her clit, her nipples pulling up into hard tips like earlier.

How hard would he hit? They wouldn't be taps. Hard enough to leave marks on her body. Maybe his paddle would have cut-outs so they'd be white in comparison. Bracing one foot on the side of the tub, she masturbated to the idea of him standing to the side, hand raising and falling to deliver a hard impact against her ass. In that one spot that made her pussy throb in pain and pleasure. The wetter she got, the more it would hurt. The more swollen she became, the more it would hurt.

Claire cried out at the thought, fingers rubbing and pressing as her hips rocked in response. The idea of him making her come from delivering hard, punishing blows to her ass made her body jerk in the water as heat spread out from where she ached to feel every brutal stroke.

No longer could she feel the ache of her sore body; it was all about the erotic fantasy of how Oz would punish her. Because when he was done with the punishment, he would fuck her.

Pushing two fingers inside her aching pussy, Claire arched with a sharp, needy cry.

He was going to make her beg as he fucked her. Make her beg to come, make her beg for his cum.

"Oh God," she whispered as she fucked herself, imagining his lean body behind hers as he took her in his club. Fucked her in front of everyone. Made her beg in front of everyone. Made her come in front of everyone.

Her orgasm made her cry out as she strained upwards.

As she sank into the water, she covered her mouth to stifle the next sound that came out.

Her last honest orgasm was so long ago she couldn't remember when. It had been with Doyle, she knew that much, but not when.

Either way, there was something heartbreaking, to her, in realizing that the man who had topped her, who just made her climax in the bath, was not the man she had thought would be her dom for the rest of her life.

And that realization broke her.

Fuck.

Fuckfuckfuckfuck. Fuuuuuuck.

Putting his hands on Claire had been a mistake. A huge mistake. Because he wanted to do it again. Replacing his hands with his dick.

His hard-on when he had been dressing her had been nothing, really. His dick happened to appreciate pretty little submissives and it thoroughly anticipated what followed aftercare, which was long, slow sex. Whatever. No big deal.

Until he recognized the tell-tale signs of a submissive responding. And fuck had she responded. Claire's entire body had snapped tight when he began to seek out pressure points. He hadn't meant to explore what made Claire Kolemann submit. But discovering what made her whimper and wet had hit all his buttons. He wasn't a hardcore sadist like his buddy, Jensen Evers, but making a sub cry and come, preferably at the same time, made his body buzz.

He bet he could make Claire cry and he wouldn't

need to flay her with a strap to do it.

The thing was – he shouldn't want to make her cry, beg and come.

Fuck, he wanted to, though.

He knocked the cordless phone sitting on his coffee table again and watched it spin lazily. "God damn it," he muttered and snatched it up. As the phone rang at the other end, he abandoned his sofa for the large window that looked out over a city covered in way too much snow.

"Yo."

"Classy."

"I'm a classy man."

"You coming tonight?" New Year's was one of his favorite nights at the club and not just because tomorrow he was hitting forty. This year things were iffy because there was a shit-ton of white stuff out there.

"No. Was going to but the weather is crap," Doyle said. "Sorry to miss it. So happy birthday and all that shit."

"Mm. Have you talked to Claire today?"

"No. When Dani wakes up from her nap, I'm taking the girls home."

Oz fought the urge to prowl and instead braced his shoulder against the cool glass. "She was at the club last night."

The rockstar drummer who was his best friend went quiet.

"And the scene was a fucked-up mess."

"How?"

"I had to end it."

"Who is he?"

Typical. Unfortunately, he couldn't have Doyle finding the guy and breaking his neck. Bad business for him and bad PR for Doyle. "I didn't have to end it because of him. She was out of control, D. Topping from the bottom, refusing to safe out, not letting my staff halt the scene. And they know better, but she was out of control. She has three weeks before she does a session lesson at the club."

The other man snorted. "She's going to hate that."

"Those are the rules. Everything is going to hinge on that day. You should talk to her, D. But be kind. I think it was her first time back since…"

Doyle sighed. "Fuck. Okay. I'll talk to her."

"I can't have you at the club that day, D."

The other man went quiet. "What do you mean by that?"

"This is punishment, buddy. Exactly how are going to react when I dole it out on your ex-wife?"

A low growl came from him. Shit. He needed to come clean in topping her. "She's never done a session lesson, Oz. I can't–"

"You're barred that night, Doyle. If you were her dom, this would be a different conversation, but you're not. I can't go easy because of who she was to you. That's unfair to everyone else, especially since a lot of people saw her yesterday."

"Fine. Fuck. Fine."

Oz rubbed his hand over the top of his head. He couldn't hide this. It wasn't fair. Not to Doyle and certainly not to Claire. Oz needed to own what he had done last night. "One more thing…"

"Mama!" Danielle's scream of delight made Claire

smile as the trio emerged from the trees separating her property from Doyle's. Her youngest ran as fast as her little legs could carry her, which wasn't fast when she was wearing purple rain boots. How crazy that when she was in Vancouver, snow had blanketed the city. Here on the other side of the water there had been a slight dusting of snow that had rapidly turned to mud.

"Dani!"

She squatted, ignoring every painful pull of muscles to catch her daughter and covered her face with kisses. "I missed you! Were you good for Daddy?"

"Pwayed dwums, mama." She waved her arms around like she was attacking a drum kit. Doyle was teaching Willow the guitar and when Dani joined them, he distracted her with his drum kit. How he stood the noise was beyond her.

As her daughter regaled her with last night's sleepover, Claire watched Doyle and Willow approach. He looked like a giant thug next to their eldest. His trademark mohawk had been cut down to something shorter. At six feet four, he was a big man who covered his muscular arms in dark tattoos that told the story of how Doyle Kolemann became Doyle Kole. He was large and in charge and their daughter looked so fragile and tiny as she held his hand, the other waving at her.

Even now, she wondered what the famous drummer had seen in her. He could've had anyone and he had picked her, loved her, married her.

Forgiven her.

Picking up Dani, she went inside with Doyle and Willow following. Boots and jackets were removed and Dani immediately ran over to play with her toys, greeting them as if it had been days instead of a night since she had seen them last.

Before she could organize the entry way, Doyle tidied up so the boots rested on a plastic mat and the coats hung on the appropriate hooks. Next he removed his biker-style boots.

Guess he was staying.

"Coffee?"

"Sounds good." He followed her into the kitchen, sitting at the island with his forearms braced on the marble they picked out together. "Are you okay?"

She paused, her gaze darting to the girls who were playing. "Fine. He called you, didn't he?"

"Mm. Show me."

"Doyle Kolemann, this is not your business anymore."

His black eyes narrowed in a way that made her glad he wasn't her enemy or her dom. The man had a fierce scowl and it always made the back of her neck tingle with the need to hit the ground running. "You bet your fucking ass this is 'my business.' You will always be 'my business,' Claire. Even without those two, you would always be 'my business' because you're fucking family. Now show me your god damn back."

"Watch your language."

"Baby, you are trying my patience."

"Fine." She stomped into the pantry and waited for him to join her. He spun her around and slid her shirt up.

"Aw, honey."

"It's not as bad as it looks."

"Baby, zebras have less stripes than you."

Cute. She turned, tugged on her shirt and pushed him out of the room. She focused on making coffee.

"He also told me what happened."

"Again. Nothing that is any of your business."

He folded his arms and stared at her. "Claire."

She copied him. "Doyle. Plus, it was nothing. Nothing."

"Mm-hm."

"Nothing happened."

"You're cute when you live in denial."

She flipped him the middle finger and his bark of laughter made her shake her head. "Why aren't you pissed and threatening to rip off appendages?"

He frowned and rubbed the back of his neck. "I don't know," he finally said quietly.

She did.

And it made her heart ache.

Oz – October 1989

"No blocking the door. You sure about the beer?"

"Yeah. I'll have one," he said, unable to look away from what was happening before him. It wasn't just the man and woman with a whip. Some guy was crawling on the floor, naked with something wrapped around his dick, a dog collar and leash connecting him to another guy wearing leather. A naked girl had her arms tied behind her back and she knelt, giving some dude the most enthusiastic blow job Oz had ever seen.

His own dick hardened as he studied every naked inch of her. Her hard nipples were pierced and something was crammed deep in her ass.

A beer appeared and a hard hand clapped him on the back. "First time, eh?" The man laughed as he shoved Oz towards a couch. He sank down, the bottle of beer forgotten as he saw another woman, also naked, on her hands and knees. Clothes pins pinched her nipples and, he frowned, was that a test tube in her ass?

Someone had drawn on her in black marker. Lewd drawings of a couple fucking. He really wanted to investigate what was on her. A guy was slapping a belt on her back and thighs. Instead of hurt, her face looked utterly blissed out.

"Oh my," Olivia whispered as she appeared beside him. Her eyes were wide, her face pale. Oz gave her a quick look, before he returned to watching the woman.

They sat there in silence, the sounds of the room filling the space: leather striking skin, cries of pleasure and moans of pain. It was a lot to take in. And he couldn't stop looking. Staring. He was staring and trying to ignore the fact that his cock was hard as fuck in his jeans.

"Avery. Right?"

Blinking, he looked away to see a guy sitting not far from him. A foot was braced on a naked woman while he drank a beer.

"What?"

"Avery brought you. Ditched you too."

"He did?"

"Oh yeah. It's a favorite game of his. What a fuckhead."

Yeah, that summed up Avery. "You know him, eh?"

"Fucking asshole," the guy muttered. "You're the first ones who didn't turn tail and run though. How do you know that dickhead?"

"Roommate. How do you know him?"

"We all have our crosses to bear. The kid is mine."

Wow. This was…awkward. He was sitting on a couch

with his roommate's dad at a sex party said roommate had ditched him at. Not quite able to maintain eye contact, Oz looked away, his gaze taking in everything.

His heart was pumping hard, his brain absorbing everything. He couldn't look away from the belt striking the woman. His heart picked up the rhythm, thumping in time to the strikes. His palms went damp, tingling with what almost felt like anticipation.

Chapter 3

"THREE BEAUTIFUL FLOWERS to brighten a snowy day. What a treat to the eyes."

Claire briefly hesitated in sipping her cup of Earl Grey tea as the familiar voice came from above and behind her. As much as she wanted to say it was a coincidence she and two girlfriends were having coffee down the street from his office, it wasn't. The location wasn't her choice either. Naomi Stefanos, a good friend, had picked the coffee shop because of its location. Naomi had a crush on Oz, but whatever she was throwing down, he was not picking up.

At his words, Naomi primped, fluffing her brown hair and batting her lashes. Subtle, she was not.

"Oz, you remember Naomi Stefanos and Heather Holt?"

"I do. Ladies," he said, his voice pleasant in such a way that Claire wondered if he really did remember them. "I'd love to be able to chat, but I'm on my way to meet a client. Claire, I'll see you later." He squeezed her shoulder and walked around their table to approach the counter. Naomi turned, blatantly staring at him while Heather fiddled with her cell phone.

Claire sipped her tea, well aware she was staring at Oscar Peters in a dark grey wool jacket that hid his ass. His voice was a familiar murmur as he made his order. The barista, a girl probably still in university, giggled at something he said. Charm and sex appeal, Oz had both.

"Fuck me, that man," Naomi said, fanning herself. "He's a panty dropper. Is he single?"

Claire was pretty sure he didn't go around promising to spank and fuck someone if he was in a relationship. She lifted a shoulder as she watched him take his coffee in a to-go cup. When he turned, the tea scalded her lip from her jerk as the look he sent her made long dormant things stir awake. It was a look that said his cock had been pressed against her ass as he almost talked her into an orgasm just by the threats of what he would do to her next time he saw her.

Yes, please, she thought reaching for a napkin to dab where her tea had splashed.

"Ladies." He nodded at them then as suddenly as he had appeared, he was gone.

"Holy God," Naomi breathed. "You are giving me that man's phone number."

"No," Claire said, attempting a new sip of her tea. Like hell she was giving Oz's number to anyone without his consent. She didn't even need to ask to know he wouldn't want Naomi phoning him. She wasn't his type.

For all her bravado and sex talk, Naomi was too vanilla for him. The thought made her smile as she ducked her head. Funny that of the three of them that was the truth. He'd be more interested in Heather than Naomi.

"Pfft," Naomi said, reaching for her dark roast. "It's not like I don't know where he works."

"Guys rarely find stalking attractive," Heather said, her eyes innocent when her friend glared at her.

"What do you know?" The question was catty and mean, typical Naomi. She lashed out when anyone, especially Heather, didn't agree with her. Claire often wondered why they put up with Naomi, but then she'd do something incredibly kind, redeeming herself.

When Heather's stepdaughter was in the hospital having her appendix removed, Naomi had constantly been there for Heather: grocery shopping, helping around the house, sitting with Hannah when Heather had to work. Hell, she had even been there for Claire during the divorce, which had been hell with two small children. Those types of moments truly out-shone her bitchy moments.

"Well, I know that guys rarely find stalking attractive," Heather repeated, blinking sweetly.

Claire snorted and covered her mouth with her hand just in case her tea tried to escape. Naomi opened her mouth, closed it, and flipped Heather the middle finger. Laughter surrounded the table a heartbeat moment.

Oh God, she needed this. Even if they were slightly stalking Oz by having coffee in North Vancouver. Friends, she thought, made things brighter. When Naomi had first suggested it, Claire had dithered. Normally with the girls not in school, grade one for Willow and preschool with Dani, Claire wouldn't have turned down the coffee date. With Doyle in town, however, the little escape was nice. Claire and Heather had taken the ferry over from Galiano Island where they both lived and met Naomi.

She told neither women about the moment with Oz. For one, explaining a BDSM club and why she was there was awkward, and for another, she wanted to keep it for herself. As much as she could since Oz had told Doyle, but that was different. A kind of "the polite thing to do was tell your best friend you had topped his former sub/ wife" thing to do. While neither women knew a damn thing about what was going on, Claire felt better spending time with them.

"Wait." Naomi leaned forward, her green eyes narrowing. "What exactly did the sexy Oscar Peters mean by seeing you later? Claire Kolemann, are you keeping secrets from your best friends?"

"Yes." Claire looked at each woman who stared at her, waiting for more information. "Yes, I am."

"Holy shit. Are you fucking him?"

"Shh." Claire waved her hand around. "And no," she whispered.

"You *are!* You slut! Tell us everything. And by everything I mean…fucking everything!"

To think a few seconds before this current conversation, Claire loved being with them. Now she wanted to flee. "I am not. Settle down, Naomi."

"No wonder he shot us that panty-melting look."

"Technically, it wasn't us," Heather said, resting her elbow on the table and cupping her chin in her hand, staring at Claire. "It was Ms. Kolemann."

"Holy shit. Does Doyle know?"

Groaning, Claire dropped her head into her hand. This was not how she had foreseen her coffee date going. *Damn it, Oscar.* This was his fault.

Him and his panty-melting looks.

Claire's cell rang just as they arrived the Tsawwassen Ferry. The line of cars just to pay said it was going to be a long afternoon of getting home. Heather dug out the phone and handed it over. Claire didn't recognize the number, but that didn't really mean anything. With two young daughters and Doyle constantly on the road, she had learned to answer all calls. "Hello?"

"Hello, beautiful flower. How are you?"

Her heart rate jack rabbited at Oz's voice. "I'm good. You?"

"Lonely. Come have dinner with me. Where are you?"

"In line to get tickets for the ferry. I can't, I'm driving Heather home." Her friend grinned and reached between the seats for her purse and a bag from her daughter's favorite store. "Just a minute. What are you doing?"

"I'm getting out so you can go do…him." Heather waggled her eyebrows as she opened the door. "I'll have Jared pick me up on the other side."

"Heather, no. Get in the car."

"Claire, when was the last time you had a date? I'm pretty sure it was before your divorce and maybe even before Dani was born. So go. Have fun."

"Seriously, get in the car." She could hear Oz chuckling on the other end. "You're not helping," she said to him. "Stop it. Heather Holt, get back in the god damn car. You can't walk from here."

"Claire Kolemann, you're going to go on a god-damn date. Say when and where. Call me later, say thank you and give me all the details." Heather slammed the door, halting any further conversation. Claire sat there as her friend wove through the cars in line with a jaunty wave over her shoulder, her full hips swaying and bright red curls bouncing with every step.

Uhm. She looked at her phone. "Just a minute, I–"

"You heard her, Claire. When and where."

She sighed. "When and where?"

"Five-thirty. My place. We'll go to from there."

"It needs to be casual, Oz. I'm not dressed for fancy."

"We'll go to Wallace's."

She hadn't been to the popular bar in a long time. A really long time. So many bands got their start there. It's where Doyle's band, Cyanide, pretty much launched from. The thought of listening to good music sounded really nice. "Okay. I'll need directions to your place, though." She waited for a car to pull ahead of her a bit so she could get out of line. When she was turned around, she dug out a scrap of paper that was an old grocery list and wrote down the directions. "You do realize if Doyle can't watch the girls…"

"Please. We both know he'll jump at the chance for a second night with them."

Her stomach fluttered at that because he made it seem like it would be all night. Doyle wouldn't say no to that, but how happy would he be about her having a date with Oz? "Still. I'm going to be really pissed if I have to get back into line, Oscar Peters."

"You won't, Claire Kolemann. See you at five-thirty."

She hung up and wiped damp hands on her thighs before she called Doyle in what was going to be the most awkward phone conversation ever. At his greeting, she cleared her throat. "Uhm, I'm going to be late."

"Is anything wrong?"

"No. I, uhm," she exhaled slowly before taking a deep breath, "have a date," she whispered. "I can come home if you have plans."

He was quiet on the other end for a while and she wondered if a lifetime of memories were rambling through him too. "No plans. Let me know if you don't make the last ferry."

Translation: if she'd be staying overnight. With another man. Who was his friend. "Doyle."

"Claire, honey, have fun."

"Are you sure? Is this weird for you because I can–"

"I shouldn't even factor into this. Do you want to talk to Willy? Dani fell asleep on the couch."

Her throat felt tight as she said yes.

I shouldn't even factor into this.

Suddenly she wanted to cancel but she wasn't sure why. Because it was complicated? Because someone could get hurt? Because she was constantly hurting her ex-husband?

Because, she realized as she let her head fall back against the seat, Oscar Peters suddenly scared the shit out of her…that's why.

With that realization, Claire drove away from the ferry terminal. Since she had a couple of hours between now and when she was seeing Oz…she was going shopping.

Oz – October 1989

"Your girl is into it too."

What? His girl? Another blink and Oz looked at Olivia beside him. Her hands gripped her knees and she was staring at the bound woman licking the man's dick while he caressed her face. Olivia's lips were parted, her cheeks flushed and when he looked further, her nipples were hard against her blouse.

"You play your cards right, kid, you'll discover the sweetest pussy is submissive pussy."

"Play my…what?"

The guy pushed his foot against the footstool woman's ass and sent her on her way. "Girl, look at me." When Olivia realized she was the girl, the guy held out his hand. Her own lifted from her knee and when he held it, he pulled her towards him. "Aren't you a sweet one?" He caressed her cheek. "On your knees, girl."

Olivia sank down and he guided her so she faced the party. "You touch her so she knows she's not alone with the chaos building within her. This is new. There's a lot to take in. It's scary, it's sexy, it's kinky, it's dirty." He smoothed his hand down her braid, rolled the elastic free, and combed his fingers through her hair. "Touch is reassuring."

Oz watched the man draw his fingers through her hair, smooth his hands over her shoulders and down her arms. "Hands behind your back, girl, and grip them together." She obeyed and her eyes fluttered close as he ran his fingers over her neck, down her breasts and back up. Oz couldn't look away.

"A new sub is dealing with a lot. The brain is processing so much: *Does that hurt? It looks like it hurts. Would it hurt me? Would that hurt feel good? Why do I want it to hurt? That rope. Do I want it? Why is my pussy soaking wet and my skin so hot? Why do I want?* All of this she's feeling without really understanding. So you touch her to reassure her, to ready her for when she's willing to play."

Oz leaned forward, his elbows on his knees as he watched the man touch Olivia.

"You watch her tells. Her lips. Is she licking them?

Are they parted? A sub's arousal is more than hard nipples and a wet cunt. It's her heart racing here." He caressed her neck. "It's the flush of her skin, the blowout of her pupils, how tight her fingers are gripping. Look at this sweet girl. Look at her waking up." His fingers combed her hair again and her head tilted back, a sigh whispering from her. "I don't need to put my hand between her legs to know she's wet and swollen. Look at her breathing. See it slow?"

"Yeah," Oz murmured as he watched the rise and fall of her breasts, her head still back.

"She's sinking into subspace. Some subs go there with pain, some with rope. For mine, it's in the prep. Once she's there, the things I can do to her."

The man slid his hands down, unbuttoning Olivia's blouse. Oz couldn't imagine the quiet girl letting anyone undress her in front of strangers, but there she knelt, a stranger sliding the fabric down her arms so her simple white bra revealed the swell of her breasts and her swollen nipples. When he slid his hands into her bra, caressing her breasts she arched, a soft sound coming from her as her knees parted beneath her skirt.

"Oh you are sweet," the man murmured in her ear, stroking her nipples until her hips shifted.

It was the most erotic thing Oz had ever seen.

"Part your legs for me, girl." She did, following the low tone. "Look how sweetly she obeys. Hands and knees, girl."

She moved fluidly and when he pressed against her shoulders, she sank down, her ass in the air. He pushed her skirt up to her hips, and moved around her, drawing her arms out so they rested on the floor. The gusset of her white panties were soaked. Oz reached out to touch but hesitated.

"Have you ever seen anyone so beautiful?"

"No." His voice was low and raspy as the man pushed her panties down her thighs. He jumped when the man slammed his hand harshly against her ass. The snap of skin, the cry she made had his own thighs tightening and his cock throbbing.

"Sweet. So sweet." He spanked her again and again, her skin turning red as she cried out, her hips jerking from the blow while her pussy wept. "It's all about listening to the needs your sub can't speak. On your knees, kid, time to listen."

He sank down and watched the other man caress Olivia's ass, between her legs and over her back. "Touch reassures the sub her dom is there. Touch her. Reassure her. Feel her. Learn her."

Oz's hand shook as he smoothed it over her back, down her neck to her hair and back up. The man spanked again and her body jerked, a sharp cry coming from her.

"Ahh, sweet girl. I hear you." The man struck that spot again and again while Oz slid his fingers through her hair. She arched deep, her head snapping up as she cried out in sheer pleasure. When he looked, he saw the man had a finger in her wet pussy, sliding and touching her. She rocked into him, her hips rolling as she let him work her. Her ass was a beautiful shade of red, her pussy so wet Oz could see it glistening around the man's wet finger. Fingers.

Oz watched, absorbing everything the guy did as he rubbed and pumped his fingers in Olivia.

"Come for me, sweet girl. Come."

Her body jerked as she cried out, ass tilting as she rocked her hips against the fingers fucking her harder. Another jerk and he watched her body tighten before relaxing as she spilled around him.

"And then you touch again. Reassure again. Do it. Don't let her come out of this alone. Some subs crave aftercare, others want you to fuck off. My girl loves a good cry after." The guy returned to the couch, leaving Oz to figure out the touching part of a girl he met a few hours ago. Olivia began to shake and there was panic. What was wrong with her?

"It's adrenaline," the guy said. "Reassure her, god damn it. Her brain is coming online and with that will come utter panic. She's naked in a room full of naked strangers. Touch, kid. Touch is vital." He got up, leaving Oz to figure it out.

He eased her skirt down because it seemed wrong to leave her ass in the air. Her skin was soft and he shifted so he was sitting on the floor. He drew her between his legs, hoping she didn't notice he was rocking a serious erection.

"Oh God," she whispered.

"Shh," he murmured, tucking her against his chest. "You're okay."

"He…I…you…"

"Liv, it's okay." He settled her bra over her breasts, ignoring the sharp points of her nipples. He did as the guy said. He touched. Smoothing his hand over her hair and over her forehead. Tears began to slide free and instead of wiping them away, he let them fall. Oz didn't know how long they sat there. It could've been a minute, it could've been an hour.

"Brock thought she'd like some water."

He took the glass and slipped the straw between Olivia's slips. When he looked up he realized she had been the footstool. "What is this?"

Not seeming bothered by her nudity, she sat down beside them and lightly stroked Olivia's hair. "Once a month, if he can, Brock will have a private party."

"No. What is *this?*" He drew a circle to encompass everyone.

"Oh, you're so new. Cute!" She leaned in and gave him a kiss. "BDSM," she said. "Do you know what that is? Bondage and discipline, domination and submission, and sadomasochism though Brock says that's a hard no at these parties. He doesn't have the space nor can he guarantee anyone's safety. It's like…game night. We get together and play. Just our games involve impact toys and fucking. Way more fun than game night."

"He called her a sub. What does that mean?"

"We like submitting control to someone else. Not all the time. Or all of us, anyway. Simon, the one on the leash, is a 24/7 slave. He likes his dom having all the control over decisions, sex, clothes. I, on the other hand, only like being topped in sex. Anyone tells me what to do at any other point and I'm going to shove my pointy-toed shoe up their ass. He likes you."

"How can you tell?"

"He didn't kick you out, keep her for himself and fuck her brains out. He would too. He liked her. He likes the sweet subs. I'm too bratty for him. What about you, cutie? Do you like brats?"

He grabbed her wrist before she could ruffle his hair. "That would be a no."

Her pupils dilated. "Understood. I'll leave you to cuddling her. I'm Dayna by the way."

"Oz."

She smiled and darted away.

"Dayna's chatty. If she bugs you just send her on her way." Brock returned, sitting on the couch and watching them. He took a sip of his drink, holding out his hand. Oz was reluctant to let Olivia go. She cast him a nervous look and at his nod, she took the man's hand. He pulled her up and onto his lap with ease. Not willing to be on the floor alone, Oz moved to the couch and watched as Brock lowered his head and began to whisper in Olivia's ear. A blush spread down her neck and across her breasts. Once again her nipples swelled beneath her bra, and her thighs squeezed together before relaxing. Brock continued to speak and her thighs shifted with her hips.

Her lips parted at whatever he was saying and his hand dipped under her skirt, making her arch.

She bit her lip, melting when the older man covered her mouth, kissing her slowly and deeply, his hand moving between her thighs. Her hand fluttered before falling to his thigh. Tongues licked and sucked, Brock muffling the noises she made as he worked his hand.

She cried out, her hand reaching down to grab his wrist beneath her skirt. Muffled cries came from her, her hips pumping and jerking and Oz knew the man was fingering her again.

"Come for me, girl." There was a bite of command in the man's voice and she arched, coming again with a cry. "Now go kiss him."

He pushed her up and towards Oz. Oz caught her as she tumbled into his lap. He brushed his thumb over her mouth, wiping away the other man's kiss then Oz lowered his head. She tasted sweet and soft, her tongue licking his.

"Straddle his lap, girl." When she did, Brock moved behind her, his hands cupping her breasts as he straddled Oz too. "Shall I tell him what you told me?" He thumbed her nipples while Oz cupped her hips. "Part of a scene is the negotiation. That's where you find out what she wants, what she doesn't want and what is a possibility. Consent, kid, is key. She liked the spanking. A lot." He peeled off her blouse and opened her bra, stripping it free. "She liked it when I played with her nipples too."

He squeezed and pinched, making Olivia jerk and writhe on his lap. Oz swore he could feel how wet she was through his jeans. Brock licked her neck, biting where the curve of her shoulder, making her cry out and buck.

"Sweet," Brock murmured as his hands slid over her stomach and between her legs. Oz could feel the man touching her, rubbing his dick. "He thinks so too," he said against her ear. "You feel that, girl? You've got two doms worked up to fuck every delicious inch of you. I love sweet, submissive ass. Would you like that, girl? Both of us fucking you?"

Her breathing quickened and her fingers dug into Oz's chest.

"You could lose both virginities at once."

Oz's hands clenched her hips as she rocked over him. He leaned forward and kissed her because to not kiss her would be a crime. Her mouth parted for his tongue as Brock rubbed her pussy. A hand curled around his neck as the kiss deepened.

Reaching up, he caught her hand, lowered it and eased it between her body and Brock's. Her hips rolled as if they were already inside of her. Brock caught her hair and tugged back hard, making her cry out. This time he had no doubt as she came over him, the wet heat of her spreading over his jeans. While Oz held her wrists and Brock held her hair, the other man tugged her head back and kissed her. Oz lowered his head and licked her nipple, wetting the tip and sucking.

"Lead her, guide her. What do you want from her? Her cunt around your dick? Her mouth? Tell her, lead her. Dominate her, kid. This sweet girl craves it."

He wanted to fuck her. Now. More though… "Lie over my lap."

She did, Brock disappearing as Oz found his stride. He eased her skirt up, caressed her ass and brought his hand down. He learned how hard he could hit her to make her squirm, make her ass lift, make her scream into the cushions. He loved watching her ass turn pink and feeling his hand burn. He flipped her onto her back, stretched out over her and kissed her. Legs wrapped around his hips and she rocked her hips into him.

"Please, please, please," she whispered.

"Tell me what you want?"

"Fuck me, please. I ache so much."

He was tempted. God, he wanted to be inside her. To see if Brock had been right about submissive pussy being the sweetest. "No."

"Oz. Please."

"Your first time isn't going to be on a couch with people around us. Hands over your head, hold the arm of the couch. Don't let go. If you let go," he paused and considered his options, "I'll stop."

He flipped her skirt up and lowered his head to discover that submissive pussy sure tasted sweet.

Chapter 4

THE DATE HAD been impulsive and utterly selfish. He was well aware what time the last ferry left. Was he a dick for scheming to get her to stay overnight? Probably, but he had zero regrets.

Waiting in the visitor parking lot of his building, Oz thanked the luck Gods that he had run into her. Putting the three-week time limit on her returning to the club was so her body could heal, but also because nothing made people want something like the forbidden.

While it wasn't his favorite thing to do, he rather enjoyed punishing bad, little subs. He was curious to see what she'd do.

A zippy compact-utility vehicle came down the ramp and he straightened. He remembered Doyle telling of the arguments between his daughters on what the color would be. Willow had wanted dark blue and Dani had wanted white. Claire had nipped the fights in the bud, Doyle said, by declaring she'd mix the two colors and go with a light metallic blue. Then she gave his friend shit for putting the decision in the hands of two girls who fought over the flavor of their toothpaste.

Oz walked towards the vehicle, a little surprised at

the hum of anticipation moving through him. When she saw him through the driver's window, she gave him a nervous little smile. He was the one who opened the door and before she could unbuckle her seatbelt, he leaned in and slanted his mouth over hers.

Slow down! Even as he tried to tell himself to ease up, he was licking and nipping her lips with his teeth. A hand grabbed onto his shoulder as he learned the shape of her mouth. Removing her hand, he shifted her arm so it was draped over the headrest of the seat. The soft sigh that escaped granted him access. His tongue slid in, tasting the sexy sweetness that was Claire. His hand found her other wrist and that arm was also stretched over her head. The instant her tongue brushed his, he wanted to bang his chest and roar like a conquering beast.

When he released her wrists, she left her arms in place, sighing as he traced her forearms, and down her upper arms. Lifting his head, he watched her bite her damp lip and arch when he palmed her breasts, squeezing and teasing until her nipples pressed through the fabric.

He wanted to tie her up like this, only with a lot less clothes on her.

Speaking of clothes, she had changed. Her jeans and long sleeved tee were gone. The green sweater was shimmery and clung to her breasts like a second skin. And how nice, she wore flowy skirt that ended just below her knees. He knew the riding boots were hers because she'd worn them earlier. Apparently, he'd noticed a lot in those few minutes of seeing her.

Leaving the seatbelt over her lap, his hand drew up the skirt before sliding between thighs that parted for him. Her cry was soft in her car as he pushed aside her panties and slid his finger inside her without any hesitation. She was wet and tight. A moan of frustration escaped when she couldn't move from the binding over her lap.

"Oscar."

She grew wetter the more his finger worked her, her hips twisting on the seat. There was a softness to her face as she sank deeper into the restrictions on her body. He loved watching a sub find her subspace. Everyone had a different moment.

Wrapping his left hand around her throat and squeezing a little, he was rewarded with her pussy squeezing tight while a slow, mellow sigh slid from her. "Say it right." Her entire body strained into the seatbelt, her cunt spilling heat around him.

"Sir," she mouthed.

He unsnapped the seatbelt and slid his hand free of the heaven between her legs. "You look very pretty, Claire."

Her eyes were unfocused when they opened. "Thank you. I wanted to look nice for you."

He ran the back of his hand down her cheek, one finger damp for her. "You already did. But thank you."

Pressing a hand against her stomach so she knew to remain sitting, Oz opened the back door to grab her jacket and purse. Next he plucked the key that still waited in the ignition. He swung her legs to the side of her seat, impulsively draping her jacket over the door. Both hands delved up her skirt. "Hips." When they lifted, he peeled her panties down and tucked them into his pocket.

He helped her slide from the vehicle and retrieved her jacket. Locking the doors, he took her hand and headed to the door separating them from the elevator.

Neither of them spoke as they went up to the eighth floor. He had considered a top floor condo, but passed on the idea. The condo was a holding pattern until he found what he was looking for. Both Doyle and Jensen Evers had plots of land that he envied. He designed homes and buildings for other people, but he'd yet to tackle his dream home. Hence the condo.

He unlocked the door and hustled her in. "Let me get my jacket, then we can head out. Are you hungry?"

She nodded as she walked into the living room, studying the grand piano that took up the main living space. "Do you play?"

"No," he said, drawing out his favorite leather jacket, having the urge to go casual tonight despite her outfit. She had asked for casual earlier and Wallace's was as casual as you could get. "It was my sister's."

Claire looked over her shoulder as she ran her fingers along the keyboard. "You have a sister?"

"Another time, okay?" He wasn't ready to talk about Kelsey.

She nodded, looking around. "How long have you lived here?"

"Two years? Three? Around there. I like the location to the club. I'm within walking distance. The drive isn't that long, but at four in the morning I just want to get into bed."

"How do you do both the club and the office?"

"I'm the boss." She snorted at his answer before noticing a painting from Jensen.

It wasn't subtle, Oz knew. The woman's illuminated back was to them and covered in brutal lash marks, rope weaving between her arms until the ends stretched out to the bottom of the canvas as if the viewer held them. In the palm of her hands was a white rose, gently cupped and at odds to the darker feel of the painting. Light shone down from above forming a triangle making you wonder just who exactly was in the shadows. Jensen was known for his blatantly erotic images. Oz had another one in his bedroom.

"She's…"

He stepped behind her and cupped her breasts. "What is she? What does she tell you?"

"That every brutal strike on her body was from love." Hands clutched the side seams of his pants as she leaned into him.

"Not cruelty?"

"No. The rose. It's perfect in her hands. Had it been pain she'd have crushed it." Her ass cushioned his hardening cock, her nipples so tight they made playing with them delightful.

"How do you know the rose wasn't put there after?"

Her head rested on his chest and she arched into his playing hands. "I just know. Was she yours?"

"No. She's Jensen's."

"The marks…"

He slid his hands down and back up, only under her sweater. Her skin was warm beneath his touch. As soft as he imagined that rose to be. She arched as he shoved her bra up and out of the way. He waited.

"Have you ever done something like that?"

Lowering his head so his lips brushed her ear, he asked, "Do you want me to?"

"I…I don't know. It's beautiful, though."

"Unzip your skirt, Claire."

She obeyed without hesitation and pushed it free of her hips.

"Hands on the piano." When she did, he stepped back and pushed her sweater up and over her head, studying her back. Still bruised. Pity. "Stay like that."

He left her naked but for her boots and went into his bedroom. He had opted against a king-sized bed so he could fit a second dresser in the room. One held clothes, the other didn't.

In the low, six-drawer dresser, he opened the top middle drawer and removed an anal plug and a bottle of lube.

He hadn't intended to play with her tonight. Not until her body was healed from her idiocy. But sometimes plans needed to change. Especially when there was a turned-on subbie in his home.

Crouching down behind her, he adjusted her legs into a wider spread, pulled her hips back and slicked the cool lube over her anus. A moan came from her and her head dropped forward, her entire body tensing.

"I'm not going to fuck you tonight," he said as he prepped the short, wide plug. Spreading apart her ass, he pushed it into place. "I'm not even going to let you come tonight."

"Oscar," she moaned, her ass pushing back to take the toy. He gave her ass a sharp snap. "Sir," she corrected in a breathy gasp.

"I don't reward bad behavior, Claire. Your body bears the marks of someone very much not ready to submit to anyone, particularly me. Until you're ready to accept my dominance, there will be no fucking and no coming."

"I'm ready!"

He drew her skirt back up. "Not yet. I promised you dinner and some music." He returned her sweater into place and slid his hands down her arms to where her fingers were trying to curl into the glossy black paint. "Just think…that could be my dick in your cute little ass. Pity." He squeezed her ass and a sound that was pleasure and pain came from her. Bruising could be a bitch.

He grabbed her jacket where he had tossed it over the breakfast bar and held it open, waiting for her to join him. It took a few minutes, but eventually she did, her steps slow and cautious as she became really aware of just what was crammed in her ass.

And what wasn't.

Fuck, this was going to be fun.

While also being hell, because he knew where he wanted his dick to be and it sure wasn't in his pants.

Oz – October 1989

"Hey, kid, this is my Kerry."

The woman wearing a man's robe was the one who had been covered in ink with a test tube in her ass and someone else using a belt on her. "Hi," she said with a sunny smile.

"Oz," he corrected, shaking her hand. "Oscar Peters. That's Olivia." Olivia was curled up on the couch, a blanket draped over her and her face soft and sleepy. "Sorry to crash your party."

"Joshua is an asshole. It's what he does," Brock rolled his eyes with a shake of his head. "His mother puts up with too much of his shit. He does this to piss me off and humiliate whomever he's gunning for." He wasn't looking at Oz but Olivia, a thoughtful look on his face. "First time he's ever done this to a girl, though. Very uncool."

Oz turned to look at Olivia. "You sure it wasn't me?"

"Yep. You got too much in your spine to make him comfortable. He'll give you shit but that's about it. Her, though…"

Sweet Olivia dragged along by her bitch of a roommate. Because Avery had turned his attention to the pretty, quiet roommate? Assholes.

"Want a beer?"

"Sure." He followed Brock into the kitchen. The party had wound down and only one couple remained. They had disappeared into the guest room and Oz could still hear them fucking. He got it. His dick had been hard all night. Dayna had left a while ago, slipping her number to him. Sexy older woman? Maybe. Probably not.

"Let's have a chat, kid." Brock slapped his shoulder. "This is a new world and it's a big fucking world."

"Pun intended?"

"Heh." Brock walked him into the living room. "Let's talk about domination and submission. Wake your girl up, she needs to know this too."

"BDSM 101?"

"Fucking-A."

Kerry curled up beside her husband and so began class. There were rules. Everything was consensual, but that didn't mean either of them had to consent to everything. He liked that. If he or anyone did anything to Olivia she didn't want, she could safe word out. When told to pick a word that wasn't no or stop, because neither word could mean that in the middle of a scene, Olivia picked nakinam, a Cree word for stop. Oz repeated it in his head: *nakinam, nakinam, nakinam.* Her cheeks were adorably pink throughout the conversation, her nipples tight little temptations he wanted to snack on.

Oz couldn't stop processing everything Brock and Kerry shared. There was a lot of information. His body felt like it was humming, an electrical charge moving through him.

"Did you two want to crash here or we can call a cab for you?"

Elbows on his knees, he glanced at the girl beside him. "This is your call. I'll accept either decision."

"I–" she rubbed a hand on her thigh, her gaze on the giant X behind them. "I guess–"

Brock stood up and wiggled a finger. "Come with me, girl. You're giving the cross big eyes."

Oz followed them over, curious himself. Brock turned her and pressed his fingers against her chest until her back was pressed against it. He crouched down and wrapped a padded cuff around her left ankle followed by her right. Before he locked her wrists into place, he had her completely naked. When her second wrist was locked into place, her eyes looked glassy and her nipples were flushed and hard.

"You're so sweet," Brock said, palming her breasts. "Will you let me play with you, girl?"

"Yes." She breathed the word out, her eyes closing as he thumbed her nipples. Brock grinned, lowered his head and sucked a nipple into his mouth. She cried out, her hands fisting and opening.

"This doesn't bother you?" Oz asked Kerry.

"No. I'm well aware I'm his. You should be learning."

Oz shoved his hands into his pockets to keep from

touching as he watched the pair. "First rule is to ensure her safety," the older man said as if he hadn't just been snacking on her breast. "Check every cuff. Are they too tight? My rule is a finger should fit in. If it's too tight, when she strains or pulls she can hurt herself. Circulation can get cut off. When we do the rope lesson, tightness is key. Our job is to restrain and restrict not constrict. You see?"

Oz nodded and slid a finger between her skin and leather so he knew the feel of it.

"Now that we have this sweet submissive at our mercy, we can do whatever we want. We can bite, pinch, clamp, strike and fuck to our hearts content. What's the word you're looking for?"

"Nakinam."

"Good. It's too soon for impact, but what did I tell you was key?"

Oz thought back over the night. "Touch."

Brock handed over a furry glove while sliding on a leather one. Oz slipped it on and ran it over Olivia's breasts. She gasped and her head fell back as he caressed the fur over her. Then Brock used his glove. Her eyes opened and her pupils were fully dilated.

"Vampire gloves." He rubbed it over Oz's hand. Tiny scratches made him look down. "Aren't they fantastic?" He stroked the tiny spikes over her breasts. Oz followed with the fur. Back and forth they went, one then the other, sometimes both. Soft little pants came from Olivia, her head tilted back and her face relaxed even though goosebumps traveled over her body. "So sweet," Brock murmured as he sank to his knees and drew the glove up the inside of her thigh, following with his tongue.

Olivia cried out when he did it to her other leg. He buried his mouth in her pussy, his gloved hand sliding to her ass, rubbing and squeezing as her gasps and cries filled the room. Oz yanked off the glove, stepped behind the cross and slid his hands over her breasts, pinching and pulling her nipples as she rode Brock's face. Her ankles were uncuffed and the man draped her legs over his shoulders as he licked, sucked, bit and rubbed.

"You don't come yet," Brock growled, looking up as his tongue flicked and circled her clit.

"No, no," she panted, hips rocking and rolling.

"You come when I say you can."

She nodded and he returned to eating her. Oz knew just how sweet she tasted. Wet and luscious, her skin soft and fragrant with her arousal, her clit a swollen bundle of nerves. "Oh. Oh!"

"No," Brock ordered and she shivered in response. He stood up and her legs slid to his hips. Oz saw his hands at his belt.

"No," Oz said, breaking in. "You don't get to fuck her."

"Oz, please," she whispered, begging.

"I said no."

Brock was lowering her legs and she sobbed, jerking against the cross. "Whoa, girl."

"I say yes."

Oz walked around and grabbed her chin, making her focus on him. "And I said no. Your first time isn't going to be at a sex party where we're all strangers. Got it?"

"Oz!"

"No. Get her off, but keep your dick in your pants."

Brock's smile was one of wolfish delight. He dropped back to his knees, spread her open and buried his fingers in her, making her scream as she came. He replaced his hand with his mouth, licking her clean. When he nodded, Oz fumbled with the buckles but finally got her free. Brock scooped her limp body up.

"Spare room it is."

Oz followed to make sure everything was good. All Brock did was pour her into the spare bed and cover her with the bedding.

"Not bad, kid." Brock slapped him on the shoulder. "Not bad."

Oz wasn't too sure. Who was he to deny what she wanted? And yet there was something strangely satisfying in not giving her what she wanted. "I have a lot of questions."

"Another day, kid. Pop that cherry because if you don't, I will." With that threat, Brock shut the door, leaving Oz in the room with a very naked, very willing girl. Dragging his hands down his face, he sat on the bed, not sure of what to do.

Did he want to fuck her? Hell yeah. But all she knew about him was his name, major, and that he had been rocking a hard-on all night because of everything. This quiet girl in her frumpy clothes was driving him crazy.

"Oz?"

"Yeah."

"Can you…I…"

Remembering the lesson about touch, he stretched out beside her and tucked her against him. "Sorry. I'm a little lost in my head." She nodded, her fingers stroking over his t-shirt. "Are you okay?"

"I think so," she whispered. "You can fuck me, you know. I don't mind."

A snort escaped. "Baby, that's the worst invitation to sex I've ever heard."

She giggled and wiggled closer. "This is a lot," she said quietly. "I've never…"

"Me neither. Although I'm pretty sure when Avery and Kendall brought us here, they weren't intending for either of us to get off on it."

"She's such a bitch. I hate her. She steals my stuff. I know it's wrong to hate someone, but she's really horrible. Why did you suddenly decide to come out? It looked like you weren't."

"Because it was obvious you didn't fit in with them and it made me suspicious. My sister had a tough time with bullies in school because she's different."

"How is she different?"

"She's like you. Quiet, soft, sweet. She doesn't like people. Groups make her nervous, which is ironic because you put her in front of a crowd of people with a piano on the stage and she comes alive."

"Did you beat the bullies up? You don't look very…" Her voice faded away and she shrugged a shoulder apologetically.

"People like Avery equate strength to the size of their muscles. But one punch to the throat and what good are all those muscles of his?"

"Thank you for coming, I mean, for being here."

Oz was fairly certain had he not been along, Brock would've plopped Olivia in a cab and sent her back to the university. "Me too. And not just because we fell down the kinky rabbit hole either. I liked talking to you earlier. I like you."

Her "oh" was very quiet.

"A lot," he murmured in her ear as he shifted her around so her back was against his chest, his erection parking itself against her cute little ass.

"Oh," she repeated. "You're very…"

"Turned on. You turn me on, Liv. You turn me on big time. Get some sleep. It's been a helluva night."

"I can…you know…suck you off if you want."

"Again. You with the sexy offers." He poked her side and she giggled. "Seriously, just ignore my dick."

"Uhm. Because it's soooo subtle." Her shrieks of laughter filled the room when he tickled her until she cried out "nakinam," bringing everything to a quiet stop.

"I like you too, Oz," she said just before she fell asleep.

Was it wrong to send Avery a thank you card? Could be worth it.

Chapter 5

ENTERING WALLACE'S, ONE would never know that it was an iconic Canadian bar. The bar looked like the kind of place her mother used to warn her about having a "reputation". The outside brick was covered in graffiti and posters declaring various events and activities throughout Vancouver, some so old they were torn and faded. The sidewalk was cracked; the location was prime just a few blocks from Lonsdale Quay Market. Unless you knew to look for it, you'd avoid it.

Inside was just as bad. Neon signs advertising beer and different alcoholic spirits covered walls that looked like they hadn't been washed since the building was built in the mid-1970s. Claire didn't even want to *think* about what coated the floor. Despite its appearance, Wallace's was crammed no matter what day of the week. Because what the bar lacked in warm, fuzzy feelings, it made up for in the caliber of music.

She had no idea how many bands had found their start here. She knew one band for certain had: Cyanide. She'd even seen the rock band play once before she had met Doyle. They still played here, most bands did even when they made it big. Wallace's was just that special.

At five-thirty in the evening the tables were filling up. If you wanted to sit, you arrived long before the first band went on at eight. That Oz found a table was surprising. Curious about who was going to play tonight, she looked at the massive booth to the side of the stage that took up an entire wall. Not recognizing anyone, she turned her attention to Oz, who was patiently watching her, relaxed in his chair.

She was very much aware of the butt plug in her ass and that she wasn't wearing any panties. The walk wasn't far from his condo but she had felt every step. With just his eyes on her, he managed to rev her heart rate up.

"What can I get you?"

Claire looked from Oz to the bar and finally their waitress. "Uhm. The house white." She never knew what to order in a bar, and wine was the safest and easiest for her.

"I'll have a Guinness and we need two menus."

Claire smoothed her hands over her skirt, not so much to straighten the fabric but to calm her trembling fingers. "How'd you get my number, by the way?"

"Your club paperwork."

She gasped and pressed a hand to her chest. "Using the club for personal reasons, Mr. Peters? I am shocked and horrified."

His smile was slow and sexy. "Desperate times."

"Are you going to the club tonight?"

His lashes lowered and her stomach fluttered with nerves and anticipation. "I have plans tonight. Kellan will keep everyone safe."

"The last ferry…"

"*You* have plans tonight too."

The room became too hot as she looked at him. "You said–"

"I said I wasn't going to fuck you or let you come. I never said I wasn't going to take you to the brink several times."

Her pussy throbbed and she flattened a hand on her stomach. "Oh," she responded, her brain flat lining. Thank God the waitress returned with menus and drinks. It gave her something to focus on other than the dom across from her. The menu was short and simple, taking up only one side of the paper. Oz scanned it quickly, deciding while she tried to make the words make sense.

"The minute you said yes, Claire, we both knew you weren't going to make the last ferry."

All she could feel was the dildo in her ass, which made her imagine what how it would feel if it was Oz instead. The words blurred as she envisioned being bent over that beautiful piano while he slowly fucked her. She wanted his hands on her: holding her in place, causing tiny little hurts, controlling her.

"What can I get you?"

"I'll have the burger, no tomatoes or ketchup, with fried onions instead and fries. Please let them know it's because of a tomato allergy. Claire?"

She blinked and looked at the waitress with no idea what to have. "Same thing."

"Tomatoes and ketchup?"

"No, thank you." Their menus were snatched up and their waitress walked away. "I didn't know you had a tomato allergy."

He nodded as he laid his hand on the table, palm up. "I'm a downer at pizza parties."

She set her hand in his and watched as he played with her fingers. "I'll make a note of it."

His lips twitched. "I appreciate that. What about you? Any allergies?"

"No. Although I'm not overly fond of shellfish."

"Check. I'm out of here."

She grinned. "They creep me out."

"How on earth can you live in B.C.?"

A shrug. It drove everyone nuts but those wee beady eyes on her dinner just ended a meal for her. Didn't matter if they weren't in the shell either. Oz covered her hand with his other hand and flipped it so her palm was up.

"Tell me about your hard limits, Claire."

Her stomach soared up and whooshed down as he rubbed his fingers over her palm to her wrist and down to her fingertips.

"No blood play, nothing involving urine or poop."

"Noted."

"I'm not big on being called names like slut, whore or cunt. Any names. I–" she exhaled and his fingers wrapped around her wrist, so she gripped him back. "My parents didn't approve of Doyle and when I refused to stop dating him they kicked me out, with a few choice names thrown at me."

"But he's so normal."

She snorted because nothing about Doyle was normal: none of his tattoos, not his job, and certainly not his kinks. "So name calling pulls me out of a scene and makes me feel afraid and vulnerable."

"Weren't you around twenty when you two met?"

"Just turned twenty-two, actually. We met at a munch."

Oz's eyebrows shot up in surprise and a blush warmed her cheeks. "Doyle went to a munch?"

It was hard to think of the rock star going to a casual meet-up to talk about BDSM. He hadn't exactly been a nobody. In 1998, Cyanide was working on their third album. Their first one in 1991 had been insanely popular, launching them from unknowns to a name. Getting up her nerve to go to a munch *and* seeing a celebrity had been overwhelming. Really overwhelming. Until she had started to talk to him and others. Jesus, he had been sexy. Staring at her with dark eyes and talking about kink with her and a man she'd learn was his mentor. When he had offered to top her, she had said yes because…duh. Gorgeous, kinky rock star? Hell yes. He had been everything her fantasies had craved and more.

Even when his addictions and demons had raged, he had been her world until he had almost died. She had been pregnant with Willow and he had overdosed. That had been her breaking point and his.

Watching him get clean had been the hardest thing she had ever witnessed. She had known he was strong and tough, but she hadn't realized how much until he went into rehab.

"How are you with multiples during sex? Another man or a woman?"

She had no idea. Doyle had never been into that. "I…I don't know."

"We'll come back to that. Any other strike it from the list? Types of play? I know you like costumes, does that ease into role play? Animal play? Baby play?"

She thought it over and shook her head. "I know some love that but it's not me."

"Let's talk pain," he said as if he was discussing the weather. His fingers stroked up her forearm, scratching down her wrist before caressing back up. She tightened her thighs to keep from squirming. "We both know your ass can take a beating, but that shit won't happen again. There was nothing sexy about what I saw in my club and it sure as fuck wasn't turning you on. When does it become more for you?"

Her shoulder rose and fell, but she found she couldn't look him in the eyes now.

"Claire. Eyes on me. Tell me what you need."

"I don't know anymore," she whispered, her eyes filling with tears.

"Okay, we'll discover that, but you will *not* control the scene again. Understood?"

She nodded and wiped her eyes with her free hand when their plates were set down. Oz pulled apart his burger to make sure there were no tomatoes at all then rebuilt it. She checked too since the last thing she wanted to do was cause an allergic reaction because of her food.

As they ate, he kept up the questions. They were explicit and she had no idea how he was able to do it in such a public place, not that anyone was really paying attention. They were just one conversation in a sea of noise.

When he set a plastic sandwich bag on the table, she met his gaze. "Go remove the plug and put it in here. We'll wash it at my place later."

Well. Oh. My. God.

Clutching her purse and the baggie, she darted for the women's bathroom. All the talk of limits gave her body a pleasant hum of arousal. It was hard to ignore how wet talk of bondage, wax, impact toys, gags, blindfolds and sex made her. Wiping away her arousal with toilet paper, she also reached back to remove the butt plug, wincing as it tugged and stretched, making her body react all over again.

She was a walking, talking thirty-two-year-old hormone. Shoving the now wrapped toy into her purse, she emerged from the stall to see that yes, she was wickedly aroused. Her cheeks were flushed and her eyes sparkled in a way they hadn't in a long time. She touched up her lipstick, pressed damp paper towels to her cheeks, and returned to the table.

Their dishes were cleared away and two glasses of water waited. Oz shifted his chair so it was beside hers and he was facing the stage. She gazed at the arm resting on the back of her chair and the man sprawled beside it. Even in black jeans and a casual white buttoned shirt, Oz had an air of something about him. She was pretty sure he came from money while also earning his own. He was also gorgeous enough that women around them, no matter their age, were checking him out. His blond hair was short and tidy, his face clean shaven.

His face had some wicked structure to it. Bold cheek bones, hard jaw and a sharp nose. He was all sharp angles and heavy lines and yet it worked. Her ex looked like he robbed convenience stores for fun. Oz looked like he wore a suit, made money and tough decisions. He wasn't delicate, but he also wasn't tough looking. He was masculine.

And dominant. Couldn't forget that. Ever. It dripped from him, which was cliché she knew. You only had to look at him for fifteen seconds to know Oscar Peters was in total control. She wondered if tough guys picked fights with him because of that confident aura.

She slipped into her seat and shivered when his hand slid over her shoulder, under her hair to her neck. His finger brushed behind her ear and her entire body melted. It gave up the battle with a silent *"take me now."* His thumb rested against the back of her neck and his fingers made a gentle but firm frame down her jaw. A little pressure had him turning her head to him and his mouth was there. The kiss was slow and deep, his tongue sliding in with ease.

She wasn't used to PDA. You didn't go around kissing a rock star in a bar like this. It just wasn't done. So this was new. And exhilarating because no one knew who either of them were and they didn't care either. Every time his tongue glided over hers, it was as if he was preparing her entire body to be taken. Somewhere drums fired like cannons, vibrating into her body. Or maybe that was just Oz's devastating kiss. His hand slid to grip the back of her neck and she really hoped it was so he could throw her over their table, flip up her skirt and fuck her in time to the hard beat coming from the band. To hell with his three weeks. *Now.*

A light squeeze and he ended the kiss.

It was one helluva kiss and she wanted more. She wanted his hands on her, his cock in her and his mouth everywhere. She wanted to taste him in the morning.

She wanted to slide onto her knees for him. That made tears burn in her eyes. *So long* a little, needy voice in her whispered. *It's been so long.*

"Shh," he whispered, cupping her head and lowering it to his shoulder. "It's okay, Claire. You're okay."

He cuddled her through the first set and when the

band took a break, he waved over their waitress and paid the bill. She liked that they didn't leave when the band was playing. Once her emotions and body settled, she realized they were really good. A gritty rock group, they played cover songs with the same rawness as they played their own songs. She made a mental note of the name, Blind Rage, to pass on to Doyle. In her mind, their name needed some work, but Doyle would know what to do.

She pushed all thoughts of rock and roll from her mind when Oz took her hand and led the way out of the bar. Once outside, he adjusted her jacket to keep out the chill and once more took her hand.

The walk to Wallace's felt like it took forever because of the plug.

Returning seemed to take even longer because she really wanted to be at Oz's place doing…whatever. The last ferry had left when she was removing the butt plug. Even if it hadn't, she was currently almost an hour from the ferry terminal and it was safe to assume she wasn't going to be home tonight.

As they approached his building, Oz pulled out his keys and let her in. There was a concierge who nodded in greeting as they walked by the reception desk. The elevator ride took hours, she was sure, as did the walk down the hall to his door.

As he locked the door behind her, he spoke. "I want you naked and on your knees."

God yes. She stripped right there and was on her knees within a heartbeat of her bra hitting the floor.

Oz – November 1989

"Some chick named Kelsey called, crying and shit. I

thought you were dating Olivia," Jesse said the minute Oz walked into the dorm room.

He didn't even pause as he dialed the familiar number, not caring about the time.

His mother's crisp "Hello" came through the line.

"It's Oscar. Is Kelsey still awake?"

His mother sighed and he knew it wasn't because he was calling at almost midnight. "She's having a bad day," she said quietly. "One moment."

Rubbing his chest, he put his back against the wall as he waited. "Ozzie?" Everything about his sister made him think of music. Even her voice had a lyrical bent to it, even when there were tears hidden in one word.

"Hey, honey. What happened?"

When she began to cry, he ground the heel of his hand over his heart. He hated when she cried. "The music, Ozzie."

"Tell me about the music, Kels," he said quietly, his eyes closing. He wished he was home so she wasn't feeling all of this alone.

"It's not playing right. I can't – I'm not *good* enough for it."

"Bullshit. Nothing about you, Kelsey Peters, is not good enough. Do you remember how long it took you to learn to ride your bike?"

"That's different. This is *music,* Ozzie."

"Kelsey Lynn Peters, that's enough. When you finally rode your bike, do you remember how you felt?"

She sniffled and her "yes," was whisper soft.

"How did it feel?"

"Like I was flying."

"You were so happy and proud. *I* was so happy and

proud. It took time, patience, a few bandages and a lot of practice. Maybe this piece is the same way. Maybe not all music is supposed to be easy for you. Maybe this one is special."

"Special?"

He nodded even though she couldn't see. "Tell me about it, honey."

"It's Schumann. His Toccata in C Major. It's *fast*. So fast. So hard. Maybe I'm not good enough. Even Mr. Robert says it's difficult."

"Robert is a talentless hack," he interrupted. He didn't like her piano teacher. Robert Pennington had the bad habit of belittling Kelsey and for Oscar that was un-acceptable. Oz understood the man was jealous. Kelsey was a freaking child prodigy when it came to music. She played the piano before she could walk, taught herself the violin when she was six, picked up a guitar at eight and was currently tackling an oboe. Music was her voice; it was an extension of her few understood. She had tried the music program at UBC but dropped out after a few months, utterly overwhelmed by the people. Not just in her classes but the very idea of how many students and staff were on campus caused her to cease music for a brief time until Oz brought her home.

Ironically, she could perform beautifully in front of an audience. As long as she didn't have to talk to anyone.

She wrote Oz letters, but mostly she sent him re-cordings of whatever she was working on. Every week he got a new cassette tape filled with everything she couldn't voice. He felt her loneliness because he wasn't there, he felt her love, he felt her wonder that he was following his dreams, he felt her pride and he felt her sadness because she was so isolated by her own anxiety.

He adored his sister, who was older than him by eleven months.

"Oscar," she whispered, scandalized, before she giggled. Her laugh was like her fingers dancing across the upper register of her piano: light and airy. "You're terrible. You shouldn't say that."

He snorted. "I'll say whatever I want about him. Tell me more about Schumann's Toccata."

He listened to every word, even the ones she didn't say. This was the first, he realized, that a piece wasn't unfolding easily for her. It was a challenge. Unknowns scared Kelsey. They made her anxious and sad.

"I'm going to come home next weekend," he said when she stopped talking.

"Really?"

"Yeah. We'll go have tea and go look for whales."

"Really?" Her voice got high and excited. "Ozzie, do you mean it?"

"Yes. It sounds like both of us need a break." He made a mental note to see if the symphony was performing. When they finally hung up, she was no longer crying and he wondered if there was a recording of the piece in the library.

His sister wasn't the only one trapped in her head. He needed a break before he broke.

Chapter 6

HER HEART THUNDERED as she looked at the cool grey of the tiles beneath her. A hand smoothed over her hair and fisted, pulling her head back so she was looking up at him. "I'm not a monster. You can kneel on the carpet. How you get there is up to you."

He released her and she listened to his shoes on the tiles and the closet door opened. The carpeted area wasn't far, just a few feet from her. She could get up, walk and sink back down or she could crawl. The choice, he had said, was hers. He walked by again, his socks silent on the floor, before disappearing from her line of sight.

While crawling seemed really attractive to her, the tile was hard and already her knees were hurting. She remembered how mad he had been the other night when he had seen the condition of her body when the scene went sideways. This felt like a test. To be honest, she really didn't *want* to crawl across the slate tiles.

Standing up, she walked from the cool hard floor to the soft carpet. The minute both feet were there, she indulged in her desire. She sank down to her knees and crawled past his small kitchen into the living room. With no idea of where, exactly, he wanted her, Claire stopped and sat back on her heels. Her hands could go anywhere, but instead of resting them on her thighs, she clasped them behind her back.

Legs straddled her thighs and once more his hand fisted in her hair, tilting her head back. "That was beautiful. Open for me." Her mouth parted at the order. His thumb glided along her lips before hooking on her lower teeth and opening her mouth further. She watched, her heart galloping recklessly in her chest, as he lifted a ball gag and eased it into place, bending over her to buckle it. "Until your body heals, there's no need of a safe word. You also developed a nasty habit of topping from the bottom. That ends tonight. Tonight is about reminding you how to surrender. The fireplace is on the other side of the piano. That's where I want you. You know how to get there."

She felt every fiber of the carpet against her hands and knees as she crawled passed his massive piano. Her tongue flicked along the rubber ball as much as she could, learning the shape of it. Gags hadn't been one of Doyle's things. Neither was crawling. By the time she was before the corner gas fireplace, her breasts felt heavy while the rest of her felt light.

His hands smoothed down her arms, untangling them from above her ass so they relaxed beside her. "As pretty as you look like that, I want you relaxed. Lift one finger to get my attention and fist either or both hands if you begin to feel anxious in anyway. Understood?" She nodded. With one last look into her eyes, he wrapped a blindfold over her. The sudden darkness made one hand impulsively fist. Instantly there was light.

Oz knelt down before her and caressed her arms.

"I'm not going anywhere. I'm going to be in this room the entire time. Sometimes I'll talk, sometimes I won't, but you won't be alone. The reason for the blindfold is because I want you focused on you: every feeling, every thought. This is about," he paused as he searched for the word, "realignment. We haven't talked about that scene nor how long it's been since you've been intimate, though I have an idea. We will. Trust me on that. But you're definitely," he tilted his hand sideways, "out of sync with your submission. You need to remember it's okay to submit, that it's more than okay to surrender control. So we start here. You are so beautiful naked and on your knees with nothing and no one throwing you ass into a scene you're not ready for. Okay?"

Her nod was a little slower this time. Once again he and the room disappeared. Funny how the darkness ramped up her nerves and she had no idea why.

Fingers gently massaged her hands from wrist to fingertips. "Let's just sit here and breathe for a while. Slow breath in. Long exhale."

She focused on his directions, on the fingers tenderly removing the tension from her hands. His voice faded to silence and her hands were lowered to her sides. The fire was warm against her back, soaking into the bruising that was still tender. She strained to hear where he was in the room, but he made no noise.

Her knowledge that he was watching her from somewhere in the room was seductive. She loved being like this for her dom. Hours would be spent kneeling beside Doyle, no matter where they were. Eventually friends stopped offering to get a chair for her or offering to move if he sat on a couch. Naomi once wanted to know why and Claire had hedged, saying it was comfortable and she didn't mind. Truth was it was comforting for her, she knew where she belonged. Plus, he was always within touching range. Doyle rarely gave excuses for her choice and eventually Claire stopped too.

But then she stopped kneeling for Doyle, or anyone.

Her first true heart-breaking moment in the realization that her relationship with Doyle was over was when she found herself sitting on the couch.

Just remembering that moment brought an ache to her chest. She wanted to rub the spot, but her arms seemed too heavy to lift. So she knelt there, felt the pain and exhaled her way through it.

The silence should've felt uncomfortable. After all, she was naked in front of a man who a week ago had really been nothing to her. He was Doyle's friend and happened to own the club she had a membership at. Instead the quiet felt as comforting as being on her knees. Was he right? Was she off-kilter?

She hadn't felt that way going into the club. Maybe nervous and anxious, but that was it. Granted, the scene had not gone how she fantasized. She expected it to be easy. A dom was a dom after all. Right?

Only…

Maybe not.

She couldn't imagine being on her knees for that man like she was now. Naked, in his home, with only the quiet between them.

Her finger twitched and at first she thought it was a simple muscle spasm. Until warm hands slid down her arms and back up to cup her neck.

"You look like you're thinking all the thoughts," Oz

said against her ear. He tilted her head back, his thumbs grazing the sides of her throat, resting where her pulse was scattering from his touch. "Are you feeling them too? It's okay to let go, Claire. I have you."

Those words made her throat feel tight. The satin of the fabric covering her eyes caught the tears as they slipped free.

"Let's just sit here and breathe again." His body was warm and strong against hers, his spread knees framing hers and his hands still on her neck. The firm touch kept scattering her thoughts before she could grab them.

I have you.

I have you.

Ihaveyou.

I

Have

You.

Oz felt the moment everything shifted for her. Her pulse settled beneath his touch and he all but felt every thought she carried slip away. Even the muscles in her jaw began to relax, accepting the intrusive presence of the gag. Instead of leaving her, he stayed behind her, his fingers smoothing her hair from her face. Such pretty hair. It wasn't a bold, coppery red like her curvy friend's. Claire's was a soft blend of light red and dark gold.

He unbuckled the strap of the gag, picked up the warm towel and without seeming to disturb her, he eased the ball free and wiped her mouth and jaw. The sigh that whispered from her made him smile. Even though it hadn't been in long, ball gags were uncomfortable. They did the job though, which for him wasn't stopping a sub from talking, but it made them unable to voice every thought or chatter to avoid those thoughts.

Caressing down her arms and back up to her shoulders, he gave a squeeze and left her kneeling on her own. Back in his armchair, he watched her breathe. He really hated the bruises on her back. If they weren't there, he could put his own marks on her, place her in his bed and spend the rest of the night fucking her until they were both exhausted.

He told himself to be patient.

She wasn't ready, no matter what she said. Her actions at the club said she was far from ready to be intimate with someone and what was a scene but complete intimacy? He really wanted to haul out the leather cuffs, but sensed it was too soon, too fast.

This wasn't supposed to be a battle for her. And it sure as shit wasn't a race for him. He kept an eye on his watch and on Claire. Timing, he learned over the years, was crucial. If he moved too fast, he could pull her from the peace she was feeling. If he moved too slow, said peace could turn on her. Either way, he knew that tonight was pivotal for her. It was a lot of firsts.

And firsts could be scary, even when someone wasn't new to kink.

He was a new element to her. He'd changed the game in the club. He'd upped the ante with inviting her out tonight, then bringing toys and negotiations to the table. Not to mention he currently had her naked in his living room.

Speaking of…

Oz left the chair and settled behind her again. His hands rested on her shoulders to let her know he was there. She had such fair skin compared to him. A devious voice in his head all but purred, *All the better to mark up* as he caressed down her arms. Lifting her hands, he set them on his thighs.

The faint freckles decorating her arms and shoulders intrigued him and he made a mental note to figure out how to work them into a future scene. "I'm releasing the blindfold," he told her. Before he could open the knot, she curved her hands over his, halting him. "I won't let you hide in the darkness, Claire." He loosened the fabric and let it fall to her lap. "We can sit here, we can have a soak in the tub, or we can curl up in my bed. Those are your only choices."

"Here."

He shifted off his knees and braced them on either side of her. Resting his elbow on one knee, he smoothed his hand over her hair. It took a few minutes for her to ease off her own knees. Claire sat with her back against him and her legs drawn up. He didn't whisper platitudes, because he was unfamiliar with how she liked her aftercare. Some subs liked words, others quiet, and some didn't want it at all. Until he and his sub became more comfortable and familiar with each other, Oz kept it simple.

"Can you talk to me?"

"I can do anything you want."

"Except fuck me."

He smiled and kissed the top of her head. "Except fuck you. What do you want to talk about?"

She shrugged, shifting so she was sideways between his legs, her body curled against his. "You pick."

Leaning back against the leg of the piano, he flipped

through stories he could tell her. Something not too complicated because he wanted her to get to know him beyond being a friend of Doyle's, but he also wanted the story to be personal. "Did Doyle ever tell you how we met?"

She shook her head, resting it on his shoulder. His fingers stroked up and down her arm as he remembered meeting the rock star. "It was a few months after he did that video for Other Side. You know the one?" He glanced down and a blush was on her cheek. A slow nod made him grin. He bet she knew the one. The video had been pretty risqué for 1996 and featured Doyle as a dom beating on three willing submissives. "Anyway, I knew the guy who was the technical advisor. Did you ever meet Jamie Hennessey?"

"Yes. He was good friends with Doyle. Nice guy. I didn't know you knew him."

"Met him a few years earlier at a sex party. Great guy although he could be a total asshole, especially when he was scening. He became Doyle's somewhat mentor and decided he needed to know more doms so Jamie had, what he called his 'dom nights only' where we'd get together, shoot the shit about anything and everything. Imagine my surprise when the new guy he brought along was Doyle Kole. I recognized him even though I'm not a massive fan of Cyanide. I was star-struck for a few minutes. At least until he opened his mouth. Then you realized just how much an asshole he could be. So full of himself. Thought he was top shit because he was Doyle Kole and we were just…guys who got turned on by kink.

"Shit, but he was greedy to know about everything. Jamie worked him hard with lessons on who was really important in a scene. It sure as hell wasn't Doyle Kole, that was for sure. Took a while to warm up to him. One day he called me to ask some questions as Jamie wasn't around. The questions were what to do if a scene went bad. He had a submissive, a girl he played with, and he triggered something in her. Freaked her out. Freaked him out. I went over and it was then that I realized he was really serious about being a dom. He wasn't Doyle Kole in that moment. He was just a guy, figuring shit out. I knew what it was like. You're just bombarded with all this information. Fantasies are firing in your brain like fireworks. I talked him through what to do and when she finally left, we sat down with a six pack and by the end of it all, we were friends."

"Sucked in by the Doyle Kolemann charm, eh?"

It was a bit more than that. There had been no charm that night. Just a guy panicking because his sub was in full-on meltdown. Oz had gone to Doyle's place for her, but he wound up staying because of Doyle. Triggers were tricky things, especially when you had no experience with them. He'd been fairly certain that Doyle was more upset by the evening then the sub. The fact that the selfish, self-indulgent rock star had given a damn changed Oz's opinion on him. Thank God, because it was a friendship that meant a lot to him. "Something like that. Then he met you. At a munch. How'd that happen?"

She plucked at the buttons on his shirt, avoiding looking at him. Reaching up, he snagged her hair in his fist and tilted her head back. Her pupils expanded and her lips parted. Claire Kolemann liked her hair being pulled. He gave another tug because her reaction was beautiful. Her coiled position relaxed somewhat, giving him a glimpse of her nipples hardening in response.

Leaning down, he licked her arched neck, sucking where her pulse leapt. Her hand fisted on his shirt as he sank his teeth into her, scoring her skin lightly. A sweet little gasp escaped and when he looked at her face, her eyes were closed and her lips trembled with each exhale.

Done with talking about her ex, Oz covered her mouth with his. His tongue boldly stroked in, staking claim. Releasing her hair, he cupped the side of her face as they kissed. Lifting his head, he ran his index finger over her damp mouth and slid it over the edge of her teeth and along the silky softness of her tongue. When her lips closed over him and she sucked and licked his fingertip, his cock hardened with the need to replace said finger.

Decisions, decisions.

Oz – November 1989

"She is a sweet thing," Brock told him as they set up the living room for this month's party. For the past four Fridays, Oz and Olivia had been coming to the man's house for what he called BDSM 101 classes.

He was discovering pieces of himself he hadn't known existed. Not just the kinky parts, but his confidence was growing. He felt it and he saw it in Olivia too. She was still quiet and soft, but she sure as shit wasn't taking any crap from her roommate.

Avery left Oz alone too. A fist to the face would do that. Not because of what he had done to Oz, but because he intended to hurt and humiliate Olivia. Why? Because she wasn't interested. Asshole.

Friday became his favorite day of the week. Not just

for all the kinky stuff Brock and Kerry were teaching him. He honestly enjoyed the older man's company. He was funny, listened to Oz when he put down limits in regards to Olivia even though it was pretty obvious Brock wanted to have sex with her.

Hell, so did Oz.

Despite a lot of fooling around this past month and Friday nights at the house, she was still a virgin. Trust, he learned, was pivotal in a dominant/submissive relationship. She was trusting him with a lot of shit and he hadn't even learned it all. The only impact toy they used was a flogger and Jesus he loved that bastard. He also hadn't used ropes on her, only bondage cuffs. Brock was taking his mentoring very seriously, which his wife thought was hilarious.

After their sessions and after the aftercare, there was some serious fooling around with Olivia. He was positive no one came as prettily as she did and he witnessed some highly intense orgasms from Kerry during "class."

"I know," Oz said, glancing over at Olivia, who wore another blouse and skirt. He was starting to love her frumpy wardrobe because it meant he got to unbutton her.

"Are you going to scene tonight?"

"Maybe. She's worried about it."

Brock locked the Saint Andrew's cross into place thanks to a couple of bolts hidden under a rug. "She is or you are? Don't hold her back, Oz."

"Or what? You'll threaten to fuck her again?"

"Or she'll walk away. You've got to listen to her, kid. Your head is so full of information, you're not hearing her."

He just didn't want to rush her. This was new for both of them but at least he wasn't coming into this as a virgin. What was that like? He watched Brock swagger up to her, backing her against the wall. Frowning, Oz watched the play between them. Her hands were pinned above her head, their hips close together as Brock spoke to her.

There was something in the way he talked to her that made her melt. It was the only word Oz could think of. Within minutes, he'd have her soft and willing and Oz felt like he was stumbling his way through this. This was a ritual. Every Friday, Brock would corner her and talk to her. Just talk.

"I don't…" His hands fisted in frustration.

"That is a forty-three-year-old man with almost fifteen years' experience of topping," Kerry said quietly as she wrapped her arm over his shoulder. "He's seen and done a lot, Oz. You're one month into this. Give it time."

"I can't do that." He flicked his hand at them. Olivia's hands were relaxed where they were pinned to the wall, her eyes unfocused as Brock spoke. When he let go, her hands remained in place, her body under his command as he gathered up her skirt, hooked his fingers in her panties and drew them down her legs. He caressed up and she arched off the wall, her pelvis pushing forward as her face showed how much she liked what he was doing.

"Give yourself time. You need to trust yourself and her. The minute you do, honey, it will click into place. What do you see when you look at her?"

"She's the sweetest girl I know."

"Do you know what he sees? The sweetest sub. And she yearns. He knows he can give her what she needs. It's not just the touching but how he touches her. He doesn't see her as fragile or sweet or virginal. He sees a girl who craves to surrender. Not just her body but her soul. For a dom like Brock, it's catnip. She doesn't need a boyfriend or a friend, Oz, she needs a dom. I know it's hard because you're new at this and he's…Brock. It's more than kinky fun, honey. At his core, Brock is a dom. And for a sub like Olivia–"

"It's catnip?"

"Watch tonight. Not the subs, but the doms. I know we're tempting but you need to see it, recognize it, and fucking embrace it. Because you have it, honey, it's just afraid."

"What's it?"

"The dominance. Let Brock scene with her. Not teach both of you, but do an actual scene with her."

He wanted to say no because he was feeling territorial and jealous because he truly couldn't do that to her. One leg was over Brock's shoulder and he was eating her out but still her arms remained up, her face so beautiful in her response. He couldn't do that. Oh, he could make her come, but that look. He hadn't seen that look since the first night.

And that, he realized, was the real reason he didn't want to scene tonight. He wanted her all soft and floaty because he knew what he was doing.

"You don't come," he heard Brock demand and Olivia nodded. Oz dropped down onto the couch, his elbows braced on his knees and his hands fisted in front of his mouth. *You don't come.* It wasn't the words or the demand, it was something else. Kerry squeezed his shoulder in sympathy.

Brock did something to her leg that made Olivia cry

out in shocked pain. "I said you don't come." He returned to her pussy. When her arms started to slide down the wall, he pinched her thigh and her arms shot back up, her body straining towards him. Brock stood up and spun her around, his hands pinning her wrists to the wall as he pushed what was no doubt a hard cock into her ass. He spoke in her ear until her fingers curled into the wall.

Oz tracked the movement, studying it. A foot knocked her feet further apart and her skirt was pulled up over her ass and her head fell against the wall as Brock kept up the words. Both wrists were captured in one hand and he untangled her braid, gathering her hair up to catch with his other hand. He bit her neck, his hips pumping with hers.

Everything the man did had a purpose, an air of something. It was intangible and it was frustrating that Oz couldn't do that.

When Brock stepped away, Olivia reached down to hold her skirt above her creamy ass, her thighs slick with arousal. Oz was pretty sure she had no memory of arriving with him.

Brock walked to the buffet covered in sex toys, grabbed an anal plug and lube, returning to Olivia. Every touch seemed to telegraph to Olivia as lube was spread over her anus and the plug pushed in. Her ass canted up even as her fingers dug into the wall. Brock was at her back again, his words for her and her alone, his touch was for her and her alone. The dom was completely focused on her as they talked.

"Jesus, it's a fucking thing of beauty when he negotiates." The woman from last time dropped down beside him. Donna? No. Diana? Dayna. "Hey kiddo, you came back."

"What about his negotiations?"

"Yes or no questions. He has a check list and that list has a list. Sex? Yes or no. Anal? Yes or no. Multiple partners? Yes or no. Pain? Yes or no. Sharp pain? Yes or no. Ropes? Yes or no. But it's like he already knows all the yes answers. I once almost came in negotiations because he's up close and personal about it. I had one guy who met over coffee. Fuck. It was like taking an exam. But Brock he touches, keeps it intimate, and that dom voice of his. Jesus, my vagina."

Dom voice? What was a dom voice? Before he could ask, Brock walked Olivia over to a chair. He sat, gave a finger snap and she sank to her knees between his legs. Kerry brought him a beer, kissed him and chatted as Olivia opened his fly with trembling fingers.

Narrowing his eyes, Oz leaned forward and decided to listen to Kerry's advice, mostly because he really didn't want to watch his girlfriend suck another man's dick. At first he thought Brock was ignoring her as he spoke to his wife, caressing her panty-clad ass. Oz saw a foot rub Olivia's thigh. When she gagged, he touched her and said something that seemed to ease her. Oz was ninety-nine-point-nine percent positive that was the first dick she'd ever had in her mouth.

Fingers slid through her hair and another word had her clasping her hands behind her back, right above the ass filled with a plug.

She was the most perfect thing Oz had ever seen even when Brock fisted his hand in her hair, holding her as he fucked her mouth until he came with a barked out "fuck!" Oz watched her swallow, her body shaking.

Another word had her daintily licking him before Brock grabbed her by her upper arms and lifted her onto his lap. She curled into him and he stroke her hair, his head bent to hers as he spoke.

His aftercare felt way different than Oz's. He wasn't coddling her or rocking her, just touching her and talking until she relaxed. She remained there, a contented little kitten. The night was still early so not everyone was there. He didn't recognize some of the people. Dayna skipped off and was talking to a guy smoking a cigarette, his attention on her. The sassy woman who had been talking to him was gone.

More negotiations?

Dayna said something and the dom barked out a laugh and spanked her bare ass hard enough to make her shriek and rub, but her nipples were hard and her eyes were sparkling. The two walked over to the cross Oz had helped set up. The man's hands wandered over her naked body while strapping her into place.

Kerry plopped onto his lap. "How're you doing, honey? You look dazed."

"Isn't that fast?"

"Dayna is a brat. Jerry loves to warm up with a good brat."

"How do they do that? Just bam—" He snapped his fingers, his hand falling onto Kerry's lap.

"Confidence. Experience. Practice on me. Tell me to get on my knees."

"On your knees."

She snorted. "Oh, honey. Don't tell me. *Tell* me. It's here." She flattened his hand on his chest. "It's that piece of you that won't take Joshua's shit. It's that piece of you that went out with a bunch of guys he hates because he wanted to protect a girl he didn't know. It's that piece of you that hates it when Brock calls you kid because that piece of you knows exactly what he's doing when he calls you that. It's the core of who you are. Do you know why Brock can put me on my knees with one look? It's because he knows that's exactly where I want to be. Where I need to be. For him, his one job in this life is to give me what I want, what I need. Sometimes it's a spanking, sometimes it's a caning and sometimes it's being on my knees while he touches me, letting me and everyone know around us that I'm his. I'm not a submissive because of him. I'm *his* submissive because of him. When I'm his submissive, I'm not his wife. Now put me on my god damn knees like you god damn mean it."

As much as he wanted to, Oz found himself struggling with everything she said. While not everything came easily to him, he couldn't figure out why this was so complicated. From what Kerry and Dayna said, this should be easy. Like having blonde hair and hazel eyes, it's who he was but damn it. At least he was finally understanding how his sister was frustrated with struggling with something she loved. Oz was in the same damn boat. He lifted Kerry off his lap gently and left the room, unable to watch Brock top Olivia any longer.

In the kitchen, he filled a glass with water and stared out the window into the backyard slowly vanishing in the night.

"How're you doing?"

At least someone hadn't called him kid. He sipped his water, feeling like an utter failure. "Okay," he somewhat lied.

"What was your name again?"

"Oz," he muttered and looked at the guy who was older than Brock. He withdrew a cola from the fridge, cracked the tab and sat down at the table, kicking out a chair for Oz. Sitting down, he waited for yet another lecture on how amazing a dom Brock was.

"Jamie. It's pretty obvious both you and your girl are new to the scene. All of us were at some point. Being new sucks. You have to learn everything. Safety precautions, knots, what kind of rope is the best, how does the equipment work, how hard do you strike, how long do you mind-fuck. There is a lot of shit going on in your head. Meanwhile, all your girl has to do is…relax and enjoy herself.

"I recommend taking some massage classes. Good for prep before a scene. Loose muscles are better than a tense body being struck. Also great for aftercare but it becomes serious fun when you learn where all the pressure points are. Now that's dirty fun. Hit up a bookstore and get a book on sailing knots. A slip knot is going to get you nowhere." He bent down, reaching into a bag at his feet and tossed Oz a coil a rope. "Practice with this. Practice knots using your leg, furniture, your girl. That means safety shears." He plunked a pair of scissors on the table that weren't the usual ones. One side was flat and the other was shorter. "Regular scissors are either going to jab your sub or won't grab the rope to cut. Always… *always* have scissors on you when you're doing bondage. Even leather cuffs because buckles can fail. Nothing kills a mood like blood or lack of circulation or having to call 911 because shit has gone south.

"Second, you have got to get your shit together. You

are one mind-fuck away from walking away and that would be tragic. There is nothing worse than smothering an intrinsic part of who you are."

Mind-fuck. He spun the scissors as he watched Jamie sip his drink, his gaze steady on Oz. "What's a mind-fuck?"

Jamie's cheeks puffed out and he leaned back in his chair. "Oh boy. It's the game. Kerry, love." He wiggled his finger and Kerry smiled as she came in.

"Hi Jamie. I didn't know you were in town."

He didn't respond. He snapped his fingers and pointed down. Instantly her knees hit the floor and she clasped her hands behind her back. Hoooolleee shit. Oz stared at Jamie in amazement.

So *that's* what Kerry meant.

Jamie stood up and walked over to a butcher block of knives. He brought them back and set it down, pulling out a knife and running his thumb along it as he looked at Kerry. At a large chef knife, he set it down went to a drawer and found one of those blade sharpener rods.

"Tell me about yourself, Oz," Jamie said as he began to sharpen the knife. Kerry's blue eyes were huge as they watched the slow slide of blade over steel, the soft grind of metal on metal.

"I'm in university taking architecture." Jamie's eyebrows rose as if surprised. "I love old buildings and how they've stood the test of time. One of my favorite things to do when I'm home is hang out in the parliament building when nothing's in session while I try to figure out how it's lasted so long. There's something magical in the history. Glass and metal is okay but it doesn't tell a story. I want to start a story with my buildings. It pisses my dad off because he designs high-rises across North America."

When he was home, he took a sketchbook into the back room while his sister played Beethoven for him. The classical music fed into his love of sketching out old buildings or redesigning new ones to look old. She said that playing the composer reminded her of him: the music could be light, could be dark, could be joyful or could be sorrowful. A lot of the weekly cassettes she set him had a Beethoven piece along with whatever she was working on.

Jamie nodded and set down his knife, leaning down to reach into his bag, pulling out a pair of metal shackles. Not padded cuffs, not leather, but old fashioned shackles. Kerry's breath quickened as the man moved behind her, locking her wrists in place. "Open." He tapped her chin and when he did he rested the key against her lower lip. "Close. Don't drop that. You don't want to drop the key, dove." Her lips closed over it.

"What you want to do," Jamie said and it took Oz a moment to realize he was talking to him, "is get yourself a good kit together. Wander through a few sex stores and if it makes your dick hard, buy it. Better yet, take your girl along and what she touches, add to the mix. You want different lengths of rope, different types of restraints, a couple of bottles of lube, box or two of condoms, a blanket for aftercare. I've got dildos and vibrators, blindfolds. Take a look." He pulled out a black scarf and wrapped it around Kerry's eyes. Oz wanted to snoop but he was entranced with what was happening before him. Jamie picked up the chair and set it behind her. He reached for the knife.

"Some of the fun is what makes their pussies melt, but what is also delicious is what scares the fuck out of them." He laid the blade over her breast and she sucked in sharply. "Such pretty skin." His voice became low and intimate. "It marks up so beautifully. And these full breasts. I love big tits on a sub. You can do so much to them. Bound with rope I swear she looks like she's going to pop like a balloon. To capture those plump nipples in a clamp? Like berries, swollen and sweet. Let's decorate these luscious tits." He set the knife on her lap and Kerry was so still that if Oz wasn't looking at her, he wouldn't recognize her. Jamie pulled out some wicked looking clamps, leaned down licked and sucked before capturing her nipple. Her shoulders hunched and a squeak came from her. "Too tight?" She nodded and Jamie flicked her before easing the pressure. "Always ask. Nothing kills a scene like unwelcome pain." He clamped her other breast, and reached for the knife.

"Now here she is. Beautiful and sweet. I can do anything I want to her. Even a cut of this knife will make her cunt wet and ready. The sharp steel against soft skin, fragility under my control, waiting for the first kiss over her skin." He drew a line over her breast with the knife and her face went slack, her thighs parting even as a whimper came from her. "A good blade will draw blood without hurting." He drew the knife over her breast, and leaned down to lick. "Sweetest fucking honey. Almost as good as her pussy."

Her nostrils were flaring as she breathed heavily, her jaw tight as she tried to hold onto the key. Jamie drew the knife down her stomach and a cry came from her when he rested it against her clit. Her stomach muscles jerked as she came.

"Fear is almost as erotic as pleasure. It's the art of the mind-fuck." He set the knife down, one he had drawn from his kit and not the one he sharpened. "Dull as fuck. Test it."

Oz picked up the knife as Jamie picked up the key that fell at her climax. He rubbed and pressed his thumb against it and it barely creased his skin.

"You dropped the key, dove. I don't think I'll fuck you after all."

"Sir," she breathed, her face flushed and relaxed.

"So pretty when she says that." He caressed her neck, unlocking her wrists from behind her only to lock them over her lap. "Now mind what I'm about to say, young Oz. Not just a sub can get mind-fucked. Now get the fuck out of here. School's out for the night. I have a sub to beat."

Leaving them alone, Oz walked into the living room, thinking over the man's words. Leaning back against the wall with his arms folded over his chest, he watched Brock and Olivia. She was tied over a leather foot stool and he was taking a sturdy paddle to her ass. He'd stop, push the anal plug back into her, fuck her with it and go back to turning her ass red. Her hands fisted and flexed, grunts of pain coming from her even as her ass lifted to the strikes.

Jamie's words began to cycle, mixed with Kerry's. Moving to a couch, he sat with his elbows on his knees and his fingers entwined and forming a bridge before his mouth, his thumbs tapping on his jaw. Jamie was right, though, he was processing so much information. He had to be aware of so much. While Olivia was having the time of her life, her sexuality opening up with every Friday session, Oz was logging serious time with his notebook.

Olivia was repositioned, her ass raised and her ankles tied to the stool. Brock delivered serious blows to her ass with a wide paddle covered in leather so her cries filled the room. It was almost a surprise when the paddling stopped. The older dom stood behind her and slid his hands down her back, up her stomach, and down to her pussy. Her cries of pain turned to pleasure as he worked her. When the man reached into his back pocket and pulled out a condom, Oz stood up. As he reached for the lube, Oz went to retrieve the scissors and rope from the kitchen. Kerry was sprawled over the table and Jamie was spanking her with a wooden spoon.

He paused only long enough to watch Brock slowly push his cock into Olivia's ass before he headed to the guest room he and Olivia shared after one of these parties. A large part of him wanted to go back to the campus, but he didn't want to leave her alone.

He had a lot of shit to work out. Watching his girlfriend get fucked wasn't going to help. Stripping down to his boxers, he stretched out on the bed and stared up at the dark ceiling, replaying every conversation tonight, including the one about the mind-fuck.

Suddenly, it seemed very important for him to decode what Jamie told him.

Chapter 7

CLAIRE COULDN'T LOOK away from Oz's eyes as he rose to his feet. He backed up to the sofa, sat down and crooked his finger. Twisting to her hands and knees, she crawled towards him. It was instinctual to stay on her knees for him.

She was so aware of her body it left her breathless.

Her lips tingled from his kiss while her tongue still felt the glide of his finger. Her aching breasts swayed with each move and her thighs rubbed together in a delicious way. He spread his legs, making room for her, his lashes shielding his eyes but not hiding them. The look he gave her made her sex throb.

Her breathing broke when his hands opened the fly of his jeans and he pulled out his cock. She couldn't look away as he stroked himself from base to tip and down again. Sucking her lower lip between her teeth, she closed the distance between them. His right hand tangled in her hair and she felt a warm rush between her legs.

"Do you come?"

She panted as she gazed up at him, her body feeling both heavy and light. "No, Sir."

"Do you get my cum?"

"No, Sir."

"I need to fuck something and since your pussy is a no-fly zone, I'll take that pretty mouth."

Yes, Sir she thought as he halted any words by pulling her head down and sliding his cock into her mouth. His hand controlled every move she made, pulling her back and pushing her down as her tongue licked and tasted him. Every time his fist tugged her hair, she felt a response between her legs. When he told her to rest her elbows on his knees, her hands up, she obeyed. The position was awkward and she grew wetter at the realization she was utterly under his control. She felt his controlled rhythm in the throb of her clit while the leather of the sofa rubbed her tender nipples in an added caress.

She sucked and licked, learning the intricate flavors of him while discovering the shape of his penis from the thick shaft to the swollen head.

The low growl that came from him made her entire body ache even as she felt herself slipping deeper with every controlling motion of her head.

He did exactly as he said. He took her mouth, fucking her to his own tempo even as her own hips rolled in response, imagining what it would be like to feel his cock everywhere. Low in her belly she felt the familiar quickening of an approaching orgasm. Her hand fisted and relaxed which only made him fuck her mouth faster before pulling her free with a wet pop. His hand wrenched her head back so painfully she felt hot spurts between her legs and over her breasts as he came on her.

It shouldn't have been erotic; it shouldn't have made her own pussy tighten and relax in her own orgasm. But it was. His cum on her breasts felt like a claiming and she felt tears slide free.

"Did my pretty little sub come?"

"Yes, Sir. Sorry, Sir. It's been a while."

"It's hard to be mad when your tits look so beautiful. Unfortunately…"

She shuddered at that one word. Anticipation and nerves making her body hum.

"Unfortunately," he repeated, quietly. "How do you punish a sub you can't spank?" He tucked himself away and rose up.

He dragged her up, and holding her hand, he pulled her into the master bathroom. He set her in the shower. It was the coldest shower ever and when she swore at him, he shoved a face cloth in her mouth and watched as the icy water rinsed away his cum. He made her hold the shower head between her legs so her own orgasm was washed away.

When she felt like a human popsicle, he ordered her to bring a towel into the living room and leave the cloth in her mouth. He set the folded towel on the floor and made her kneel, her body air drying while he turned on the television. He ignored her for sports highlights.

The jerk.

More fool her, she loved every moment of it.

The last time she slept with a man had been the night before she effectively killed her marriage.

Oz's mattress was firm and the sheets smelled of man and fabric softener. The bed wasn't large, the queen-size giving it a sense of intimacy especially when Oz slid in behind her. Her heart fluttered nervously and her palms were damp as she tucked them under her pillow. He turned off the bedside lamp and the room plunged into darkness, adding to her nerves. Her entire body went still and she tried to muffle her gasp when five feet, ten inches of naked man settled against her back.

Suddenly her nudity felt different than earlier when he had been clothed. Her hand made a nervous fist under the pillow as his hard cock pressed into the softness of her ass.

"On your stomach, Claire. You're so tense you're going to snap."

She rolled onto her stomach and a shiver moved through her as he ran his hand up and down her back, lightly caressing the gradually fading marks. "I'm sorry," she whispered, burying her face in the pillow.

"Why? You have nothing to apologize for." He leaned down and kissed the top of her spine, his fingers beginning to lightly massage her shoulders. "Do you know why we're both naked? Why I didn't give you a shirt or leave my boxers on?"

"Because you're a sadist?"

His chuckle seemed to vibrate through her back. "Because all night you've been naked and vulnerable with me. How can I not do the same? That and there will never be clothing between us in this bed." His fingers caressed down her ribs to where her breasts were pillowed against the bed. "If I want to play with you, nothing is in my way. If I want to fuck you, nothing will slow that need down." He stroked down her side to her hip and over her ass. "I want your skin against mine, your body warm against mine and when you wear my marks, they'll be the only thing between us."

His fingers slid down and her thighs parted, giving

him access to her pussy. "Feel how wet you are already?"

She nodded as he stroked and teased her. "Oz," she breathed his name just to say it and was rewarded with him pushing two fingers into her, making her cry out.

"Do you have any idea how desperate I am to fuck you? Slide your left leg up, love, and open for me."

She did and he teased inside her, strong fingers gliding within her.

"Your brain may be hesitating, which is natural, but this body doesn't know the meaning. Such a hungry little submissive, aren't you?"

"Yes," she moaned, her hips rocking in time to his touch. Her eyes rolled behind her closed lids when he pushed his fingers deeper and found that one spot that made her cry out. "Oz, Sir."

"Oh I like that," he said against her ear, rubbing and pressing until her legs tried to close. "Say it again, sub."

Her pussy clenched. "Oz. Sir." She grunted when a third finger pushed in.

"Again," he breathed. Against her thigh, his cock was heavy and hard, his fingers relentlessly working her until the pillow swallowed her cries.

"Oz. Sir. I'm going to come."

"I know."

Oh. *Oh God.* "You said…"

"I want you to come, love. I want you to fall asleep with your pussy aching for my cock, your thighs slick from the orgasm I allow and the feel of my fingers deep in your cunt. I want you to come, love, so you know I can make you feel this good. I want you to come, Claire, and feel everything."

He bit her, the pain of it shocking her. Her entire

body shuddered at the sensation so different from the erotic strokes. She cried out, her ass lifting and her pussy squeezing his fingers. Her hips rolled and she came, her body released by his words to do so.

He eased her onto her side, his fingers damp on her hip and his cock hard against her ass. "One day your bruising will be gone." His hand slid between her legs, caressing her tender clit. "The day it is, I am going to fuck you. But first, I'm going to put my marks on you and when I do, you'll beg for release. Show me how you beg, Claire."

Oh sweet Jesus, she thought as he began to pinch not just her clit but her swollen labia and her stomach. Reaching down, he lifted her leg and draped it over his before he returned to the teasing touches and punishing pinches. She couldn't remember the last time she had been aroused this much and considering her earlier orgasms, one allowed and the other not, that was saying quite a bit.

Her body writhed under his touch, her cries of pain and pleasure melding into pure need. Everything felt swollen and tender. She craved the cock she pushed back into. One hand began to rub her clit while the other pinched up her stomach and all over one breast. "Oz. Please."

"What?"

"Fuck me. God, just fuck me."

"No." He tweaked her nipple and slowly massaged her throbbing clit.

She cried out in frustration and need. Did she sound sulky? She feared she did but all she wanted was for him to ease the constant arousal. "Please!"

"No," he whispered in her ear, "but I like hearing you beg for my cock. I'm still not going to fuck you."

A sob escaped. "Sir, I ache. I ache for you."

"Tell me where, love."

She flattened a hand over her heart that was trying to pound its way out of her chest. "I'm going to come."

"No, you're not. You can take more."

"No. Pleasepleaseplease."

"You sound so pretty. What does my sub need?"

She cried out at the words, feeling them swell deep within her. "You!"

His whispered "Come" was at odds of her scream. Released, she came, her body shuddering and shaking. Tears slid free because it felt so good. Her legs slid shut, trapping his hand.

His other arm folded over her breasts sore from his pinches, his hand flattening over her galloping heart. Claire gripped that arm, needing to hold onto something as everything cracked apart.

My sub. That one pronoun was slashing her open. She didn't deserve it. She was a terrible sub. A horrible one. For the first time, she felt the other dom's marks and they hurt. A deep pain that told just how wretched a sub she was.

Oz held her as she cried, painful sobs dragged from deep inside where all her betrayals lived. "Oz."

"I'm here, love. I'm here."

"Oz." All she could say was his name. He deserved a better sub, one worthy of him. She was the worst sub. The worst. She had betrayed every dom before him and she'd do the same to him. She didn't want to hurt him.

"Ah love, you'll be okay. Let it out, sweetheart. Let it

all out."

Oz – November 1989

The soft press of breasts against his ribs as a warm, naked body curled up against him woke him up. A slender leg rested on his while Olivia nestled her head into shoulder with a quiet sigh. Fingers feathered over the back of his hand that rested on his stomach. "I wish you were awake," she said in a quiet whisper, her breath warm against his skin. "There's so much I want to tell you. Everywhere I was struck hurts but it's not pain. It's like I'm feeling my skin and body for the first time. How can I feel this alive after someone hit me? I wish…" Her monologue faded to silence, leaving him wondering what she wished.

He could ask. Instead, he lowered his other hand from behind his head and fisted his hand in her hair, pulling back with enough force to make her gasp in surprise. He pulled her to her back and covered her body. He wished he could see her face as swift pants of air brushed over his mouth.

"You were a bad girl tonight, Olivia." Where this voice came from, he had no idea: low and deep, filled with threads of jealousy and something else. Like when Jamie told Kerry she didn't want to drop the key. "You didn't just come without permission, you fucked without permission."

He wondered how long it would take to erase the sight of Brock pushing his dick into her ass. Maybe never.

She went still beneath him, although short breaths continued to escape. "Did you think I didn't know?"

"I…sorry," she whispered. "One–"

"I don't want excuses. What's the one rule, Olivia?"

"He doesn't get to fuck me."

"What did he do?"

Her swallow was audible in the room. "But it was my ass. It doesn't count."

"Baby, if his dick's in you, he's fucking you. It counts. Roll over."

He climbed off her and flipped on the bedside light. Her slender body shifted but not before he saw that her dusky nipples were tight and her eyes were wide.

There were marks of impact on her body. Nothing overly serious – red areas, especially on her ass. Straddling her thighs, he studied her body. He guided his hands over the tender zones and the sound of her sucking in her breath was rather delicious. Curious, he pressed his thumbs into a spot on her ass. A sharp cry came from her as she writhed beneath him. Leaning down, he pressed his mouth against her ear, smiling when he heard her panting into the pillow. "That was fun. Shall we do that again?"

"Yes. No. I don't…"

"Yes, it is." Straightening, he let his hands slide over her until she tensed from him finding a tender place. Then he pressed on it. He imagined it was like when you touched a fresh bruise. Another cry rang from her and she gripped the pillow with both hands. "Are you wet, Olivia?"

She nodded and he pinched her waist. She jerked as if to get away from him. "I want words, Olivia."

"Yes," she said, shrieking when he pinched the same spot. "Yes, I am wet."

"Show me." He eased off her, flattening his hand on

her shoulders so she didn't roll over. He let her figure out how to show him, her legs sliding open. "That shows me nothing. Show me."

A hand released the pillow, vanished under her body and reappeared with her fingers glistening. Sexy. Leaning down, he sucked her fingers, his tongue caressing her as he removed every silky drop. He lowered her hand to the pillow, straddled her thighs and returned to finding the sore spots.

Every gasp and cry made his cock throb. Two more times he made her show him how wet she was. Her hips rocked into the bed and tiny cries of pain blurred into a combination of pain and pleasure.

She never looked so sexy. Brushing her straight dark hair out of the way, he leaned down to kiss the back of her neck, his tongue tasting the saltiness of her skin while his erection pressed into her ass. When he nipped her ear, her body gave a tiny jerk while she moaned. "It's too bad you were so bad earlier, because I'd be sliding my dick into you right now."

"Oscar, please. I'll be good. I promise."

"That's pretty," he said, borrowing the phrase from both Jamie and Brock. "But not pretty enough. On your hands and knees." Climbing off the bed, Oz watched her rise up. Her head hung down, her hair cascading to the mattress and blocking his view. Reaching under, he tapped her chin. "Head up."

She flicked her hair out of her face, revealing flushed cheeks and lips swollen from biting. Her breasts quivered and she trembled, her nipples swollen and tight.

"The next time Brock or anyone else puts their dick in you, I walk. I don't care if it's your mouth, your ass, or your cunt. What do you say?"

"No," she answered.

His hand connected with her ass in a stinging blow. His palm tingled as a yelp came from her. "Try again. What do you say?"

She licked her lips. "Nakinam."

"That's right. In negotiations, it's a hard limit. Since you look perfect like this, let's get this out of the way. I've decided I'm not going to let you come." A groan came from her and her head fell forward, making him battle a grin. She was so adorable. She really was. He gave her ass another swat and she raised her head up. "Why aren't I?"

"Because I was a bad girl."

"Mmhm. This is going to sting," he said, bringing his hand down eight more times on her already tender ass. He caressed her bottom, his hand sliding between her legs to her slick pussy. "Off the bed."

It took her a few minutes to catch her breath before she crawled to the edge and stood up. Her eyes weren't quite focusing and it was such a pretty sight.

"Down."

He really wanted to master that snap of Jamie's, but not tonight. He helped her sink to her knees, and he shoved his shorts down. Her dark eyes went wide as he slid his hand along his cock. "Now." He sat on the bed and gazed at the sight before him. She was stunning. "Suck."

Chapter 8

HE WANTED TO get shit-faced drunk, which was rather surprising as he wasn't much of a drinker. Sitting on a leather sofa on the viewing level, Oz gazed down into the pit. He watched the various scenes without really seeing. Good thing his head of security, Kellan Brandt, was keeping an eye on everyone.

His head was definitely not in the game.

His thoughts were focused on the redhead who had left his place a week ago and he hadn't been able to see since. His night off had coincided with Doyle having some rock and roll thing in California. An awards show? He couldn't remember. All he knew was that Claire wouldn't leave the kids overnight with her teenage baby-sitter, even if the girl's mother stayed over too.

He couldn't blame her, but Christ, he missed seeing her. Phone calls weren't entirely satisfying because he could sense her unwillingness to participate in phone sex when her kids were in the house. Again, he understood.

It was the missing her that was throwing him for a loop.

With one foot braced on the low, metal and wood coffee table, he watched as a dom beat the hell out of his submissive, both of them having a great time.

It wasn't even like he could do a full-fledged scene with Claire. He was the one who had put the three-week time frame on her so he couldn't exactly go back on that.

"You look like a man in need of a drink." A bottled water was tossed onto his lap and he picked it up as Jensen Evers sat down beside him.

"I wasn't expecting you tonight."

The sadist shrugged, propping his feet on the table. "Kelly is visiting family in Seattle and I was bored. I think she's going to move back."

That was surprising. Kelly was both Jensen's model and sub. "Really? Why?" He studied his friend. "Haven't seen her around lately and you haven't sought out a S and M night. Things okay?"

"Nope." Jensen sipped his own bottled water. "They haven't been for a while."

"What's going on?"

"She fell in love."

Well, that was unexpected. "Let me guess…someone in Seattle?"

"Five points to the architect. She's promised to stay to help me find a new girl."

"Accommodating of her."

Jensen shrugged as his gaze moved over the women in the club. "It actually is. You know of any little pain honeys looking?"

"Let me check." Rolling to his feet, he went into his office and grabbed his list of submissives who were looking for dominants. Returning to the couch, he flipped open the file. He wrote the names down on a separate list and handed it over. Jensen didn't look, just shoved the paper into the back pocket of his jeans. "There are newbies coming in too. They haven't filled in their final paperwork or completed orientation. I'm doing a session lesson."

"No shit. Been a while since we had an infraction."

Oz took a long sip of water, his gaze roaming over the pit. "With Claire Kolemann."

"Fuck off. Does Doyle know?"

"Mm." He found himself not wanting to share more of his time with Claire. He wanted to hoard it to himself. Bad enough Doyle knew. Bad enough? Christ. Those words alone… "She stayed over last night."

Jensen began to cough, his water spraying just enough to have him covering his mouth with his hand. Well, that felt good. Oz took a calm sip of his drink, his attention on the couples playing.

Some nights he wished to be like his members. Come in, do a scene with his sub, and enjoy the night. A night where he didn't have to keep an eye on everyone under his roof. Not that he resented the responsibility. It was one of the reasons why he opened Edge. He did, however, wish for the partial anonymity of simply being a member.

"At your place?"

"Well, I certainly didn't leave her at my neighbors'."

"Again I find myself asking the previous question: does Doyle know?"

"Mm."

Jensen made the same soundless noise "Is that why he hasn't been around?"

Fuck. Leaning back, he looked at his friend who simply shook his head. "Seriously, Oscar? Claire? Out of all the submissives who walk through the door, you hook up with her?"

The way Jensen said that was as if there was a line-up of willing girls at his office door. His reality was far from that.

He was a man who worked during the day, was home long enough to eat, change his clothes, maybe grab a nap, then be at the club until all hours of the night. That already limited the number of women willing to put up with that. Add being dominant and the window shrank considerably.

Claire had already been with one guy who wasn't around, so the odds were pretty slim whatever was going on with her wouldn't go beyond a scene or two.

It bothered him how much that irritated him.

While he'd known her when she was married, he had known her as Doyle's wife. They hadn't been friends beyond that relationship, so he was now discovering all kinds of interesting things about her. He wanted to learn more. He wanted to know her outside the kink world.

When was the last time that had happened?

He tapped his fingers on the arm of the sofa as he thought of the subs over he'd had the years. There were a lot. An obscene number of girls had come into his world, and the minute they wanted more, he gently shuffled them on their way, because he didn't want the emotional mess. "How long were you and Kelly together?"

Jensen didn't even have to think. "Six years."

Six years. That was two years longer than the club had been open. Oz couldn't even name five subs he had played with in that time. "And your sub before that?"

"Allison was five years. Is there a point to this conversation?"

"You know all their names, don't you?"

"There's not a long list. Kelly, Ally," he lifted his fingers as he gave names. "Georgia, Diana and Liz. And Liz was–" He waggled his hand back and forth. "She was a switch. She was also my modern art teacher at ACAD." He grinned as he clasped his hands over his chest, his gaze clearly on the past.

"Did she teach a young Jensen more than art?"

"Yes. Yes, she did."

"Who suffered with you the longest?"

Jensen's grin turned wicked. "Kelly. And before you ask, Diana was the shortest relationship. Two years because when I moved here, she wasn't willing to give up her dreams to follow me and nor should she. She's a pediatric surgeon in Toronto at Sick Kids now. Married. Nice guy."

"Jesus, you keep in touch with them?"

Jensen lowered his feet from the table and rested his elbows on his knees. "I do. These are masochists. I like to know they're okay with their doms, if they have one. Do they feel safe? If they don't, do they need help? Our kink can not just maim, it can kill. Just because they're no longer mine doesn't mean I don't care. Each of those relationships was intense. They weren't just my little pain sluts, but my employees too. Where are you going with this, Oscar?"

He was just taking stock of his life. "Aside from the first two, I barely remember their faces."

"You're so full of pity shit."

"Okay. You name one of my subs. And by that I mean someone around for a long time."

Jensen pursed his lips, his eyes narrowing. Oz could

almost see the other man mentally flipping through images of women in his mind.

"Stop," Oz said, lifting his hand. "It wasn't a real challenge."

"Okay. I don't know where you're going with this, but if that's the case, you better damn well make sure that Claire isn't forgettable or else it won't just be Doyle beating the shit out of you."

Who, Oz wondered, would deliver the most pain? Doyle, who was built like tank, or the artistic sadist?

He really didn't want to find out.

"Moooom," the soft whisper against her ear caused Claire's eyes to open. It took a moment to make out the shape of Willow beside her bed, elbows digging into the mattress.

"Hi, baby, bad dream?" She lifted the duvet. Her oldest crawled in and snuggled against her. "Do you want to tell me?"

"I couldn't find you or Daddy. I called and called but you weren't there. Every time someone turned, it wasn't you or Daddy." Willow played with Claire's fingers, her whispers not as quiet as she probably thought they were.

When Doyle went away, it used to be easier when the girls were little. It wasn't like being left for a weekend. Sometimes it was a year. The first month or so were always the hardest because suddenly he wasn't there. Now that Willow was older, she was realizing her dad was gone for a long, long time. Even Dani was realizing that when Dad went away, he was far away. He couldn't always call them at bedtime because of time zones.

Cyanide didn't have a tour planned at the moment as

they were battling their way through an album, but there were still times when he made an appearance at an event or talk show or he'd barricade himself with the band to write music. It didn't help that the guys didn't always get along.

It had taken Claire a few years to realize just how dysfunctional the band really was. She didn't hear the stories anymore, but Doyle never went on tour excited to play music for their fans. His sporadic calls were filled with rage towards Jace Jennings, the lead singer, and frustration with Anderson Reeve's addictions, which was ironic considering Doyle used to be ass-deep in drugs and alcohol too. It was as if by becoming sober, Doyle's bullshit barometer with the band broke.

"You know that will never happen, right? Your dad and I will always come when you call. Even when you're old and we're old, we'll come."

"I know," Willow whispered. "When's Daddy coming home?"

"Should we go look at the calendar?"

Her daughter nodded and they slipped out of bed. Scooping her up, Claire carried her downstairs. Willow's arms were surprisingly strong as she wrapped them around Claire's neck, her cheek resting on her shoulder. Willow was getting heavy and one day she wouldn't be able to lift her. The knowledge left a tiny ache in her heart. Her baby was growing up.

A light was always on in the kitchen and not just for the girls. The island's streetlights were few and far between. The night could get spooky, especially when the big, bad drummer was away. Walking over to the calendar the girls had picked out for Doyle, Claire put a finger on the day. "He left on Sunday, today is Wednesday. When is he home?"

"Sunday," Willow said. "That's a long time, Mom."

"Not that long because you have school and you wouldn't see him during those hours if he was here. Right?"

Her daughter nodded as they headed back upstairs.

"Friday you have piano, so you wouldn't see him. Saturday is swimming. You're so busy that time will fly." She tucked her daughter back into the canopy bed that was Claire's as a kid.

"Can I listen to Dad until I fall asleep?"

"Absolutely." She pressed play on the small CD player beside the bed. The strums of a guitar drifted from the speaker, and Doyle began to sing a song he wrote when Willow was a baby. He called it The Goodnight Song. Claire loved his deep bass voice when he sang. The drums were his first love, and he saved the singing just for his girls.

Smoothing her hand down Willow's hair, she listened to her daughter's sweet voice blend with her father's raspy one. Gradually Willow stopped singing while the song kept replaying. When her deep breathing told Claire she was asleep, she stood and left Doyle's voice playing. She checked on Dani, who slept so deeply, it had riddled her with massive anxiety for the longest time. Dani didn't move and make sleepy sounds like her sister, so Claire always waited until she was positive her daughter was simply sleeping. She also never made it through the song once, which was nice.

Potty training was hell during the night, though.

Knowing her girls were fast asleep, Claire returned to

her bedroom and reached for her cell phone. Coverage on the island was spotty, but she wasn't looking to make a call. Instead, she opened the calendar. She didn't know time could crawl until Oz had banned her from the club for three weeks. She hadn't even considered returning until she couldn't. Now it was all she thought about.

"I'm going to make you come, Claire. With my hands and with my paddle, I'm going to make you scream. Make you beg. Make you come. I'm going to put you on that bench again and show you how good the pain can be. When you're slick and swollen from all your cum, I'm going to fill your pussy and fuck you until you beg me for my cum."

His words were embedded in her memory. Along with the feel of his body against her and his hands on her breasts.

Two weeks. Two more weeks.

She was gazing at the date when a text message quietly lit up her screen as she turned it off the ringer at night.

It was a long fucking night. A sadist threatened to tear me to pieces because of you. Someone fucked in the bathroom and this happened. A photo appeared of a sink ripped off the wall, broken tiles on the floor and water everywhere. *It's four in the fucking morning and you're on a fucking island so no ferries are running. Plus two more weeks before you can come to the god damn club.*

Rolling onto her side, she debated the one-sided conversation from Oz. She could simply set her phone down and go to sleep, instead she responded.

You're the one who said three weeks.

OZ: What are you doing up?

Willow had a nightmare.

OZ: She ok?

She's already asleep. Why the threat?

OZ: Because I'm an asshole and he knows it.

Would you really show up at my door at four in the morning?

OZ: In a heartbeat. Maybe I'll buy a boat. Or a plane.

Can you fly?

OZ: Not yet.

A boat is probably cheaper.

OZ: Planes are faster. Go to bed, Claire.

You too. Good night, Oz.

OZ: Good night, sweetheart.

Tucking her phone close, Claire stared at the conversation, running her finger over the words *Planes are faster.* Funny how three simple words made her heart beat a little bit faster while her stomach fluttered with what she discovered was anticipation.

Oz – November 1989

Oz was exhausted as he stepped onto the first ferry heading to Vancouver Island. Dragging himself away from Olivia after their night had been a challenge. He tried to convince himself to take a later ferry, but that wasn't fair to those expecting him. He hadn't really slept, there hadn't been much point. The cab he had arranged to pick him up at Brock's place had shown up at five so he'd have enough time for the ferry.

Damn, he was tired.

Stretching out on one of the bins that housed life jackets, he tucked his backpack under his head, set his sunglasses in place and shut his eyes. With just over an hour and half of cruising time, he was determined to get some sleep. Too bad last night played over and over.

For the first time, he felt like he wasn't sucking at this. The blowjob hadn't been long, his dick far too happy to be inside Olivia, even if it was just her mouth. Jesus, orgasming in her?

He bent his left leg so it wasn't obvious he was hard.

Time to think of something else, Peters. As much as he wanted to rehash spanking her and the gentle torture, he needed to refocus his brain. Trapped on a ferry with a hard-on wasn't his idea of a good time.

Going home was bittersweet.

There were constant questions from his father: how were his classes, how were his marks, how was this professor or that, or any number of replayed conversations. There was also Kelsey.

He missed his sister. Phone calls, her tapes and infrequent visits home didn't fill the gap where she lived. It's why he bought tickets for the orchestra Monday evening. First it would get Kelsey out of her safety zone of the house, but it was also just the two of them. The symphony was a surprise for her. The part that made him sad was that she wouldn't have plans to cancel. His sister was more than reclusive. She was like a lighthouse: a beautiful light trapped in a tower.

He worried about her. He always worried about her.

Oz knew he would always worry about her.

Growing up, he always felt she needed more in her life than music. Not that she wasn't amazing with the music, but once their parents realized how gifted she was, they built her entire world and worth on her music.

He was well aware of the irony that on Monday he was taking her to the symphony and during winter break he was going to take her to the ballet, which also centered around music, but it was about showing her the world beyond her music room, even if that world was the city.

One day he'd make enough money that he could show her the world. Yes, their parents were wealthy, but they weren't going to give him cash to visit places like London to hear the London Philharmonic Orchestra or to the Salzburg Festival, the home of her beloved Mozart. Hell, he even wanted to take her to New York so she could see Julliard. Not so much to show her how her life could've been, but because she deserved to see everything, experience everything.

Music spoke to Kelsey in ways people didn't, but there was so much more for her to see than the glass bubble their parents had placed her in.

Sometimes he resented their parents for the cage they put her in, even though that's where Kelsey felt the safest.

He loved and adored his older sister, and wanted the world for her.

One day, he hoped to show her everything. For now, it would be the Victoria Symphony and a night of Beethoven and her Mozart.

With his eyes closed and the fresh air on his face, Oz nodded off, waking when the ferry pulled into the terminal. At least he could sleep more since he had an hour-long bus ride into the city.

He could've had someone meet him here but it was way too early. Why have someone get up at the crack of dawn when the bus would get him where he needed to go? Once the bus arrived and he collapsed into a seat, a

smile appeared.
He was almost home. Damn, he missed this place.

Chapter 9

HER THREE-YEAR-OLD was melting down over socks. The entire day was a series of tantrums. When the mother of Willow's friend offered a playdate after swimming, Claire had envied her elder daughter's escape.

A nap was eminent for Dani.

Hell – for both of them.

It was days like this that she wished Doyle was around more. There was no winning an argument with a toddler: not over pooping in her potty instead of her pull-ups, which was an earlier tantrum because she wanted to wear her unicorn panties, not over purple socks instead of white or red, which matched her outfit, not over breakfast. There was no winning, period.

She loved her daughter, but fuck she was tired.

Claire watched Dani try to pull off the hated sock without much success because she was standing. Her poor little bug. Poor little bug's mom.

When the doorbell rang, she didn't know if she was relieved or irritated. A bit of both. Shoving her hand through her hair, Claire left Dani to her battle.

If someone told her to guess who was standing on her front porch, she never would've guessed Oscar Peters.

Blinking, she stared at the attractive man gazing at her. He looked as tired as she felt. He hadn't shaved that morning so dark gold whiskers covered his jaw and his hair was slightly messy. "Oz."

Behind her, the screams and cries grew closer as Dani followed. His eyes went wide, shifting to her daughter. "This is a bad time."

Actually, it wasn't. It was such a relief to see him, she wanted to collapse against him as Dani did at her feet. Bending down, Claire scooped up her daughter.

"It's nap time," she said.

"No," Dani said as she rubbed her face on the shoulder of her sweater and her neck, smearing tears, drool and snot everywhere. The glamorous life. "Not tiyod, mama."

"Yes," she mouthed at Oz and nodded her head. He stepped inside and toed off his shoes, shrugging off his wool jacket. "It's a tough day, right, baby?"

"Tough day," she said, tucking her thumb into her mouth, something she only did when she was at the end of her rope. Not "tiyod" at all. "I don't yike my socks," she told Oz, lifting her foot.

"But they're such lovely socks," he said, pinching her toes.

"Not poople. Want poople socks, mama. Who's dat?"

"His name is Oz."

"Funny name, mama." Dani didn't sound amused, just cranky.

Claire grinned and Oz chuckled. "Come on in. Let me put her down."

"No!" Her daughter shrieked in her ear. "Not tiyod. No down!"

She lifted one finger to him and headed to Dani's

room, a new meltdown happening. Some days.

Instead of depositing her daughter in her bed, Claire collapsed into the purple armchair tucked in the book corner. The screams melted into hiccups and sobs. Rubbing Dani's back, she rested her cheek on the soft black hair.

"Not tiyod," Dani repeated around a yawn.

"I know. So we'll just have a little quiet time instead, okay?"

Her daughter nodded. They sat there until Dani's breathing evened out and her tense little body was relaxed and heavy. There was something about having her daughter fall asleep on her that filled up her heart. Pressing her lips to the crown of Dani's head, her gaze shifted to the doorway where there was movement. Oz leaned against the doorframe, his arms loosely crossed over his chest as he watched them.

His wink made something catch and flutter in her chest.

Easily shifting her hold, Claire stood up and carried Danielle to her bed. The tiny girl was utterly relaxed as she slept without twitching a muscle. "Love of my life," she whispered. Kissing Willow's forehead, Claire wiped away the damp tracks on her daughter's cheeks away.

At the door, Oz took her hand, turned and led the way to her bedroom.

For a moment, she wondered how he knew where it was until she remembered that years ago he had visited Doyle.

"What are you doing?"

"Your little queen isn't the only one in need of a nap."

"But…"

"Get into bed, Claire." He grabbed the bottom of his sweater and pulled it off, revealing a thin white t-shirt that rose to bare his stomach.

Too tired to argue, she crawled into bed. She was surprised when he joined her. Oz tucked her against his chest and sighed.

"Do you need a nap too?" she asked. She covering the hand resting on her stomach. It was nice to hold onto someone.

"Yes. And I don't need anyone to tell me that either."

His body was warm and solid behind hers. She couldn't help remember the other night, sleeping naked with him. After she had cried all over him, he continued the erotic assault on her body, ending with her laying beneath him. He had slowly stroked his cock along the seam of her ass. His hands had pinned hers to his bed and her ankles had been tied together, his lips against her ear as he told her all the ways he was going to fuck her. She had been so aroused but unable to find relief because of her legs bound so tight she couldn't rub her clit on the bed. Instead, she had felt him and the unyielding wetness against her clenched thighs. When he finally came all over her back, she had been mindless and lost in her need for him. She had fallen asleep with need clawing her from the inside out, his seed on her skin and his body wrapped around hers.

She had felt owned and worshipped.

In the morning, he had lowered her to her knees and filled her mouth with his cock and when he had once more spilled himself all over her breasts, Claire felt as if he had claimed every inch of her. In his shower, he'd washed each of those inches with a tenderness that made her throat ache.

The man had bolts embedded in the tiles and he made use of them with handcuffs, making her watch as he washed himself. By the end of it, he had been hard again and she was wet with need because his hands sliding over his wet skin was beyond sexy.

A hand braced by her head, he had looked into her eyes as he masturbated, the water cascading over them. As much as Claire wanted to see him come, she hadn't been able to break eye contact. When he finally came, he kissed her and she had tasted promises. With the same hand, he had slid two fingers into her and her own orgasm had been a welcome relief.

Climbing into her car to come home had been so hard.

It was the best date of her life.

Now he was here.

Flipping over so they were chest to chest, she pressed her nose into his neck drawing the scent of him into her soul. He caressed up her back to her shoulders, and down to her waist, the clasp of her bra now open. Sneaky.

It gave him unencumbered access to her back. His hand slid up, bunching up her sweater, until his fingers tangled in her hair and he pulled her head back. His mouth took hers, the kiss slow and sensual. Every caress of his tongue made her melt and crave more. Her leg bent and hooked over his hip so she could get closer to him.

He rolled them so he was over her and a slow sigh escaped when he pushed her sweater and bra up and away, the cotton of his shirt warm against her skin. His mouth returned, his kisses no longer slow but deeper. Claire slid her fingers into his hair as she returned the hungry kisses. She loved the hardness of his body against the softness of hers. The way his chest flattened her breasts, how firm his stomach was against hers, the press of his swollen cock where she ached.

"I didn't come here for this," he whispered, his mouth centimeters from hers.

"I know." She wanted to ask him why he had but realized she didn't care. He could've delivered her mail and she'd be happy to see him. She ran her hand down his whisker-covered jaw, enjoying the way he felt against her skin. "Kiss me, Oscar, so I'll taste you when you're not here."

He did.

This wasn't hunger or passion; it was something more. Everything in her rose up to meet the bold strokes his tongue and the rolls of his hips. She gasped as he licked, sucked and nipped down her neck, his hands curling around her wrists and lowering them down until she gripped the headboard.

When he scraped his teeth over one nipple, Claire arched with a cry. So much teeth as he nipped, tugged and bit hard enough to make her stomach jump in response.

Hands and mouth were everywhere as he made his way down, stripping off her jeans and panties. Her eyes snapped open as his mouth landed right where she ached for him. His tongue, the slight beard, his lips, all made her moan. He lifted his head and looked over his shoulder.

"It's fine. Don't stop. Please don't stop."

Thumbs spread her open and Oz lowered his mouth

to her. His tongue on her clit made her cry out his name and arch, her fingers clenching hard. He licked, sucked, fucked and kissed her with his mouth until her orgasm pulsed through her.

He gazed at her, his eyelids heavy and his eyes filled with heat. "Look at you, sexy and satiated." He spanked her pussy hard enough to make her flinch. He braced his arm on the other side of her and gazed down at her.

He rubbed a knuckle over her pussy, teasing and tormenting her. The little smirk of his lips said he knew what he was doing to her. When he nudged his bent finger into her, she gasped at the sensation as it glided down from clit then nudged her anus. Claire bit her lip as he pressed the knuckle in, causing her hips to roll and her body to arch.

"Beautiful," he murmured. He leaned down and drew the flat of his tongue over a swollen nipple, teasing as he prodded her. Once more her hands found her headboard, hanging on as he tormented her. "Very beautiful. Roll over and bend your knees."

She was helpless to disobey. His hand glided up her back, his fingers sliding over the remnants of her night at Edge. He caressed over her ass, down her thigh and up the inside of her leg until his fingers rubbed her pussy. The pillow swallowed her moan as he dipped his fingers into her, working her until her body moved like was he inside her.

"Jesus, these piss me off," he growled, his hands stroking over the fading marks. His hand fisted in her hair and yanked her head back, making her cry out at the stinging pain even as her pussy softened for him. "Tell me your safe word, Claire."

Her heart pounded hard in her chest, a combination of arousal and fear because of his voice. There was so much anger and fierceness in it. "Sunshine."

"What is your safe word, Claire?"

"Sunshine."

"Say your safe word, Claire."

Tears burned in her eyes and her throat grew tight as she repeated, "Sunshine." Over and over he made her say it. Behind her closed eyes, the tears slipped free. He pulled her hair so she was almost bowed, the pain not comfortable.

"What is your god damn safe word?"

"Sunshine, sunshine. It's sunshine."

"You ever come into my house again with no intention of using it and you will not like what you unleash. You will be banned. Your membership will be revoked in such a way it will be heard throughout the community. I will walk away without looking back. No apologies, no tears, nothing will make me acknowledge you. I will forgive you anything but that. Are we clear, Claire?"

She nodded, unable to look away from the raw anger in his eyes. "Yes. We're clear, Sir."

The backs of his fingers were gentle as they stroked over her cheek, despite the hint of violence in the air. "Do you need an invite to an S&M night?"

Her stomach dropped at the idea. She and Doyle had never gone to one of the dark nights of the club. The thought of lying to him made her queasy. "I don't know," she whispered. "Maybe."

Oz – November 1989

Bracing himself on the doorframe, Oz listened to

Kelsey play. She was lost in the notes, the concentration on her face almost fierce. Her fingers made him think of magic, which was fair because everything about his sister made him think fairy princess. There was something otherworldly and delicate about her as she played without looking down. Suddenly discordant notes rammed the air as she repeatedly slammed her fists down on the keys, a sound of utter frustration erupting from her.

Bolting into the room, he wrapped his arms around her when she swiped the sheet music off the piano. "Hey, hey, hey," he crooned quietly as she tried to slam her back against him. It took a few minutes for her to settle down, the fight going out of her as if strings had been cut.

"Ozzie?" Her head fell forward. She sounded so lost and young. "Is it really you?"

"It's really me." He rested his cheek on her head, looking at the door when their mother appeared. The relief at seeing him there and being the one to handle one of Kelsey's meltdowns made him swallow down a lifetime of curses. His parents were perfectly content when Kelsey played beautifully and was their idea of perfection. Moments like this, however, left them in the shitty parents column.

Kelsey tilted her head back and he shifted so she saw him. She looked so tired. "Ozzie." Her eyes closed and a weary sigh escaped. "You're really here."

"I have a surprise for you. It's in my backpack."

She scrambled away from him, hurrying over to where his bag rested. Like a child at Christmas, she rooted through his clothes and shaving bag. In the front pocket, she found the envelope with Kelsey written on it. Sitting on the bench, he smiled as she pulled out the card with colorful butterflies on it. She opened it and stared at the tickets.

"We're going to the symphony?"

"Yes, we are. On Monday, it's just you and me."

She gasped and clutched the tickets to her chest. She leapt to her feet and ran over to him, throwing her arms around him. "You are the best brother in the entire world."

"I know. Have you had breakfast yet?"

"Maybe?"

He laughed as he stood up. "Shall we go have breakfast somewhere?"

"Yes!" She twirled like a child before she bolted out of the music room, her joy contagious. Grabbing his bag, he went to his bedroom. Until now, he hadn't realized how much he needed to come home. Here there was no stress about school or worries about his relationship with Olivia. Here everything was simple: breakfast, a weekend in the city he loved and an unofficial long weekend with his sister.

Chapter 10

THE BED SHIFTED and Claire turned her head as Oz wandered into her bathroom. A few minutes later, he returned with a folded towel and a bottle in his hands. With practiced ease, he flicked the towel out beside her. "I want you on the towel, laying on your stomach."

Claire eased over. The bed dipped slightly, and he straddled her ass, the worn denim of his jeans cool against her skin. He gathered up the hair he had been pulling earlier so it no longer rested on her back. When his hands touched her, they were slick. She wondered where he had found the oil because she didn't remember having any. The thought faded away because…damn.

Fingers that could hurt dug into muscles, pressing and kneading until she swore her body was melting away. The quiet between them was comforting. Against the towel, her nipples beaded in response to his touch. The nervous flutter in her belly almost made her feel giddy because this man who had been so fierce a few minutes ago was now tender in the aftercare. She sighed, turning her face into her pillow when those strong fingers began to massage her ass. Each squeeze and caress stirred her body that craved him so much.

"You don't hide your responses to me, girl. Ever."

It was funny how one word, said in a certain tone, could trigger the need to surrender everything. Resting her cheek on the pillow she was clutching, she kept her eyes shut as his thumbs dug into to the tender skin where her thighs met her ass. His weight shifted and he massaged down her thighs and back up. On the second journey up her back, he draped her arms over her pillow before returning to the deep massage. Every muscle was limp and she felt like she was floating.

Oz adjusted the pillow and when his strong, slick fingers slid to her breasts, her moan came from somewhere deep in her. He kept the same measured pressure over her breasts and nipples before returning to her back. Between her legs she was slick and ready, but she was so lulled from the massage she could barely move.

"Tell me about Edge. What were you looking for that night?" He squeezed and stroked her hips, her thighs, her ass and back up her back.

"I wanted to forget," she said. His hands stilled before resuming a gentler massage.

"Forget what?"

"That the dom wasn't mine. That I didn't need the release. That he wasn't Doyle."

"So you had him beat the crap out of you? As what? Punishment or proof?"

Claire sighed. "Both?"

"Only it didn't work, did it?"

"No," she responded truthfully. "I'm sorry, Oz."

"I'm not the only one you need to apologize to, Claire."

She swallowed and nodded.

"What do you need? Not in a scene, but in your dom."

Opening her eyes, she thought over the question. The massage never paused but she felt each finger on her skin like it was inside her, touching all the lonely places that yearned to be owned, to be claimed. She wanted that so very badly.

She couldn't explain it, her answers tangling up inside.

Oz's hands caressed down her arms and curled around her wrists like living manacles. "That felt complicated. Shall I tell you about me and what I *need*?"

Claire nodded, her hands fisting slightly before she made them relax. "Yes." He climbed off her, giving her ass a soft pat. Her breath caught in her chest when he stretched out on top of her, every naked inch of him. His chest with the smattering of fine hair was firm against her back, his stomach curving along the swell of her ass and his hard cock settled right against her sex, a heavy brand that made her ache to feel him slide inside her. His weight should've been too much. Instead her eyes closed as something akin to peace flowed through her.

"You already know my hard limit around safe words and I'll tell you why soon. Not today, though. Today is about you and I." His voice was low against her ear, adding to the intimacy. "My sub knows that when I set a lengthy punishment of, say three weeks, it isn't to make her feel abandoned but because she needs something. Maybe there's a hurt that needs to heal. Maybe there's fragile trust that needs to be strengthened. Maybe she needs that time to feel, really feel, what being my submissive entails. I won't break a promise to my submissive, even if it's three weeks of no sex, no orgasms, no scenes, because I need her to trust that I have control of the situation when she doesn't."

Her heart thundered at those words, at the meaning behind this current banishment from the club.

"I have two careers and they're selfish, demanding mistresses. That doesn't mean I'm a workaholic, just busy. I have brilliant staff working for me because at the end of the day, and the beginning, my submissive always comes first. If in the middle of a work day, or night, she calls me for whatever reason: to talk, to hold, to fuck, or to beat, I can quietly walk away. I am never unreachable, though for one week in the summer it gets tricky because I have an annual fishing trip with Jensen. Not to say she's not welcome, but this is definitely a group of guys getting their fishing on. That week is rewarded because a few weeks later we're back on the boat for a week of debauchery. Have you ever been tied to a mast, the salt air caressing your naked skin while you're alternately being beat and fucked?"

Her heart raced at the words. "No," she whispered, her hands unfurling as her fingers went limp at the image.

"The sun on your skin as you lay on the deck, hands cuffed to your collar as a dom fucks your cunt, one fucks your mouth and one is in your ass? A week dedicated to submissives unencumbered by anything, and their doms focused entirely on them?" Her breathing grew ragged and she was so aware of the cock notched along her pussy, his skin growing slick from her response.

"No," she repeated in a softer voice.

"I haven't gone for a few years. It's not something I take casual subs to. It's not about fun or even fucking.

It's about strengthening the bond between my submissive and I. It's an affirmation of what she means to me and what I mean to her. I am a selfish dominant. I want it all from my submissive. I don't just want her surrender, I crave it. My submissive is mine and she will never doubt it. I don't need a slave or someone tending my every need, nor do I need to control her every moment, but I do need her to belong to me. A scene may begin or end with me putting a collar on her neck." His tongue traced the back of her neck as if there was a collar there.

"You like that," he murmured against her ear. "The idea of a collar. Have you worn one?"

"No," she breathed into the pillow. She wanted to though. What would it be like to have tangible proof on her body that she belonged to someone? Something others would see and know someone owned her body and soul?

"Tell me how it looks it your mind, Claire. Is it pretty? Is it functional? Delicate chains linked together or sturdy leather that can't break? Leather," he whispered against her ear, his cock growing slicker from her body as her pussy softened at the thought. Did he know that the idea of his collar made her body ready for him? Not just to be fucked, but conquered?

"But leather isn't practical, is it? Leather is for a scene. Because my sub would wear my collar all the time. When she's getting coffee with girlfriends, when she's having a shitty day and stuck in traffic, she'll feel me there. Always."

She moaned, her head sinking down as his cock slid along her. Jesus. The idea.

"My submissive is mine," Oz reminded her. "Even

when I'm not before her, beside her or behind her, she is mine. She trusts in that knowledge, thrives with it, because she knows that means I'm hers too. I am her dom and only hers. She needs never doubt that, even with all the subs running around the club and under my care, she knows I am hers. She owns me as much as I own her."

His cock slid along her pussy, her body aching to be claimed, to be owned. The quiet was broken by their breaths as they moved together, delicate thrusts that told her he was aroused as her.

"I would own you, Claire," he breathed against her ear. "Heart, body and soul, you would be mine. Mine to protect, mine to cherish. I'm going to come on you, Claire. You have a choice of where. I can't get you pregnant and I'm clean as per club rules. I can come over your cunt or your ass. Pick."

"Cunt," she answered.

"Do you know why I'm going to come on you?" She nodded, tears sliding free. "Tell me, love."

"Yours," she mouthed, unable to voice it because it was a terrifying word.

"Mine," he said, agreeing with her.

She gasped. She felt his warmth spurt over her, sliding over her as his body held hers down. She began to shake, not with the need to come but with the need to believe.

Where the hell had he come from? This man who seemed like the dom of her dreams.

His legs slid to the outside of hers, drawing her own closed as if to hold his cum against her. His cock was soft and damp on her ass and he wrapped her in a masculine cocoon. He held her until the tears dried up. He left her long enough to dress them both. The stained towel disappeared and she tucked a hand between her thighs where she could feel her panties growing damp from the remnant of his orgasm.

He crouched beside the bed and brushed aside her hair. "Do you want me to stay or go?"

Both made her panic. She grabbed his hand and slipped it between her thighs. "Stay. Please."

His thumb feathered over her forehead while both of their hands were nestled against where he had come.

"Why isn't this weird for you? Me being Doyle's ex."

He grinned, a cocky smirk. "Who said that? I doubt myself constantly because it's a friendship that means the world to me. The idea of losing it hurts." Her heart clenched at that. Maybe the submissive he spoke of hadn't been her. Maybe it was all bullshit. "But you're not his anymore. You both didn't just walk away from each other, you burned the bridge to ashes, then salted the earth. We all know that if not for the girls, he'd have walked away completely. And that would've been a loss for both of you. But you're not his. I told you, Claire, I'm selfish. I'm an extremely selfish dom. I keep what's mine."

"Am I yours?"

"Only you can answer that and we're not quite there yet. I may be selfish, but I'm patient."

"What if I'm not?"

"You tell me that our relationship isn't want you want or need. You look me in the eye and end things. It will suck, it will hurt and it will scare you. But we both deserve better. Doyle and you deserved better. Every day begins and ends with you as mine. That's why I'm selfish. No one fucks her but me, no one comes in her but me. So if you're mine and you pull that shit on me like you did Doyle, things will end. But that's why you did it, isn't it?"

Of course he knew. He was Doyle's best friend. Her marriage to Doyle had survived years of alcohol and drug addiction. They survived him being gone for long periods of time. They hadn't survived him being sober. It wasn't anything he'd done or not done, or on her. They simply couldn't weather everything. He had been her husband, her dom and her best friend, and the only way she could see freeing them both from the quicksand of their marriage was to sleep with someone else. Not just anyone but the one person Doyle hated more than anyone – his band mate, the lead singer of Cyanide, Jace Jennings. It had been stupid and reckless, the move of a desperate woman who didn't know how to sever a dead relationship.

She had regretted it instantly. Before Doyle found them. "I didn't know what else to do, Oscar."

"Now you know. I'm a grown man, Claire. I can handle learning that this," he flicked a finger between them, "isn't working for you."

Only it did. On so many levels. She glanced away from his calm hazel eyes to their hands.

"Turning you on here," he squeezed her sex gently, "doesn't mean this works for you. I'm going ask again and I want a truthful answer. Do you want me to stay or go?"

"Stay," she whispered, this time without any hesitation. His smile was sweet as he leaned over her and kissed her, slowly and deeply, his hand still cupping her.

"Is it okay to park in your driveway? I'm currently on the side of the road and I don't want to block anyone."

"You can park in the garage."

He winked, gave her another squeeze before he left.

Reaching up, she slid her hand along her throat, recalling his talk of collars. She heard the garage door open and she thought of what Oz said. She didn't belong to a man who no longer lived here. One she hurt and punished because she didn't know what else to do.

"Fuck." She reached for the phone and piece of paper with the hotel number on it. "Mr. Kolemann's room please." When asked, she gave her name, well aware there was an accepted calls list wherever he went. The phone rang and rang before bouncing her back to the front desk. She left a message saying it wasn't vital and she'd talk to him tomorrow when he was home.

Apologizing to him could wait because she had no idea what to say. She had apologized before, but maybe it hadn't been enough.

How did you say sorry for doing what she'd done? Could she?

Oz – November 1989

"Hi."

Oz looked up from his text book at the quiet greeting. He had taken to studying in the library because his dorm room was constant noise from his asshole roommates. Exams were well over a month away, but he wasn't one to cram the week or two before. Plus, this got him out of his dorm room.

Olivia stood beside the table, clutching a book. She looked pretty with her shiny, straight hair tucked behind her ears and her cheeks flushed from being outside. "Hi." Automatically, he glanced at his watch to make sure he wasn't late for their night at Brock's. "Have a seat."

Setting her book on the table, she sat across from

him and fidgeted with aligning it just right. Oz studied the girl across from him, her attention locked on her book. "Do you mind if we don't go to Brock's tonight?"

"No. Did something come up?"

She shook her head, peeking at him from beneath her bangs. "I just want to spend some time with you." Her smile was shaky from nerves, adding to her cuteness.

"I'd like that." Her smile blossomed into something beautiful. "Anything you want to do in particular?"

"No. You pick."

He checked his watch again and flipped his books shut. "How about a movie? That seems like a Friday night thing to do." They went to her dorm first, where she changed into something she felt was date night-worthy, a light purple dress and her favorite pair of flats. At his place, he swapped his jeans for slacks and his faded t-shirt for the same button-up shirt he wore to the symphony with Kelsey on Monday.

This was, he realized, their first official date. Something every other couple did that didn't involve ropes or domination or lectures. It was a nice change.

Oz decided to splurge on a nice dinner for them. Nothing over the top that would make Olivia feel uncomfortable or wonder how a university student who didn't work could afford fancy. He had yet to explain his childhood to Olivia.

It was an eye-opening realization – to discover how little they knew about each other's life beyond the university and their lessons with Brock. As they waited for their food to arrive, he studied the woman across the table from him. "Do you have brothers or sisters?"

She looked surprised at the question. Reaching for

her glass of water, she took a sip and nodded. "I have an older sister and a younger brother. You have a sister right?"

"My older sister, Kelsey. She's a pianist." She was more than that but it was the easiest to explain.

"Is she good?"

"She's amazing."

"Really? Where does she play?"

"She'll do private recitals her music teacher arranges. Company parties, weddings, private parties. She suffers anxiety and it prevents her from playing with an orchestra or symphony. That doesn't keep her from loving the music. When I went home on the weekend, I took her to the Victoria Symphony."

Olivia's gaze dropped down to rearrange her cutlery. "My sister is pregnant with her second child."

That made him smile. "So you're Aunt Olivia."

"I guess. We're not very close. How was the symphony? I've never been to anything like that."

"It's not my slice of pie, but Kelsey loved it so it was worth it. Mostly it was nice to get home. Even though it's just across the water, I don't get back often." He planned to do more because Kelsey was struggling with the latest piece and his parents never really knew how to deal with her when she was frustrated. It was almost as if she couldn't understand why the music wasn't easy when every other piece was. "What did you wind up doing on the weekend?"

Olivia's eyes went a little wide and she looked around. They really didn't talk about their lives, he realized, if him asking about her weekend surprised her. Jesus.

What had they been doing this past month?

He knew how to make her come but had no idea how she passed her time between when they returned to the campus and when they left the following week.

What a prick.

What an absolutely selfish prick he was.

Their food arrived. A vegetarian pasta for her and a steak for him. He dug into his steak with relish. It was nice to not dine on campus food for a change. While it wasn't the best steak of his entire life, it was the best one lately. Taking a sip of his beer, he noticed Olivia wasn't eating, more like she was just rearranging the pasta and vegetables on her plate. She was quieter than usual but how did you judge an introvert's talkativeness? There was also something extremely fragile about her tonight, more so than her usual delicateness.

"Are you okay?"

She nodded and stabbed a yellow pepper with a lack of enthusiasm.

For someone who had suggested they just hang out tonight, he got the feeling she really didn't want to be here. "Did you want to go Brock's place? I could phone him and tell him plans changed."

There was a tiny flinch around her eyes and she shook her head. "No. This is fun."

"Really? Because I feel like this is your definition of hell."

"No, honestly. This is fun."

Uh-huh. He was pretty sure that whatever words were going through her head, fun wasn't high on the list. Oz found his appetite fleeing as he watched her misery grow until neither of them were eating. Nudging his plate out of the way, Oz placed his elbow on the table and rested his chin in his hand as he studied the miserable girl across from him. "Olivia."

Her shoulders hunched at her name and she peeked up at him through her lashes, reminding him of someone about to be scolded for being bad. He searched for the right words and her dark eyes flooded with tears. She grabbed her napkin and held it over her mouth as if to muffle a sob. Holy shit, what was going on?

"Liv," he said quietly and moved to the other side of the table. Her eyes, shiny from tears, tracked him. "Hey, tell me what's wrong?" Tell him so he could fix it.

She shook her head, still clutching the napkin to her mouth. "You're going to be so mad," she said.

"Why?"

There was little she could do to make him mad.

She continued shaking her head, whispering into the napkin, "I had sex with Brock."

Chapter 11

SOME CONVERSATIONS YOU absolutely didn't want to have with your ex-husband. Especially when he was coming off spending a couple of weeks with his bandmates. He didn't have the best relationship with the four other men. However, Doyle absolutely hated the lead singer, Jace Jennings, so when he had to spend an inordinate amount of time with him, her ex was cranky.

As she walked through the trees that separated their two properties, Claire struggled with what she was going to say. She had put off talking to him last night since he arrived in a pissy mood. Tonight she couldn't delay for much longer because if the girls hadn't mentioned Oz spending the day with them on Saturday, they would. They were spending the week with Doyle and secret keepers they were not.

Folding her arms over her chest, her restless fingers plucked at the side seams of her Icelandic-style wool sweater. She really didn't want to have this conversation with Doyle. Just the thought of talking to him about Oz and everything made her anxious and nauseous.

Doyle's house came into view and she could see the faint light in Danielle's room that stayed on all night shining like a beacon. The closer she drew to the front door, the more she wanted to turn around and go home. Only she couldn't. Chickening out wasn't an option. For one, Doyle deserved to know what was happening and for another, she needed to do this. Not that there would be repercussions. All Oz said was that based upon her and Doyle's past, he deserved to know and she needed to tell.

Before she knew it, she was standing on Doyle's front step. Light flickered from the living room off the entryway so she knew he was downstairs. Taking a deep breath, she looked over her shoulder towards her own home. Fuck. Exhaling, she lifted her hand and knocked on the door. When Doyle's large body filled the doorway, Claire found her shoulders hunching up like their daughters did when they were feeling guilty. Crap.

"Claire? Is everything okay?"

She forced herself to unfold her arms. "I need to talk to you. May I come in?"

His black eyebrows rose but he stepped aside letting her in. What she thought was the television on was actually a cheerful fire burning in the river rock fireplace he had. A glass of ginger ale rested beside a thriller hardcover face down on the coffee table. She stared at the soda fizzing away. Once upon a time it was a glass of hard alcohol, vodka or bourbon, depending on his mood. "Can I get you something to drink?"

"No, I'm okay. Thank you," she said slowly, still staring at the golden liquid. She wondered how his sobriety was going. She didn't ask because she always feared it would set him off: either with hitting a bottle, popping a pill, or simply being defensive.

"It's virgin," he said, his voice droll.

Wow. She felt shitty all of a sudden. "I know." It was only a partial lie but she was relieved to know there wasn't rye added to it.

"Liar."

He sat down at the other end of the leather sofa, one heavily muscled and tattooed arm resting on the back. Jesus, he was a beautiful bastard, even with that ridiculous short mohawk. No wonder groupies adored him. It wasn't that he was big and muscular, his arms covered in tattoos from shoulders to fingers. His beauty wasn't delicate or pretty, it was raw and masculine. Anyone in the know would recognize that he was a dominant alpha male. It clung to him like a potent, sexy aura. Now that he wasn't drunk or stoned, he had even more impact.

Looking at him didn't make her heart flutter anymore. Her palms didn't tingle with the need to touch him and she didn't have the compulsion to sink to her knees before him. She found that heart-breaking because she had loved him so much.

She still loved him and always would but it wasn't the same love. It was an affection in her chest where good memories blended with bad, a distant blur of the love that created their daughters. "I don't know…" She licked her lips and looked away from his face, her gaze dropping to the thumb that rhythmically tapped on the back cushion. Not out of irritation or impatience, but because there always seemed to be some kind of rhythm in his head. "I don't know how to begin."

"With the truth."

Three little words that had the power to give her a painful punch to the chest. The truth. "On Saturday, Oz showed up and spent the day with me and the girls."

Doyle bent his arm and propped his head on his fist, hiding the various drums inked between the knuckles of his right hand. His other hand had beat tattooed into the flesh. Most thought it was for what he did to his drums, she knew otherwise.

"How was that for you?"

The question was unexpected. Resting her head against the back of the couch, she thought over her answer. Did she tell him that opening her door and finding Oz there made her heart vibrate in excitement and joy? Or how a simple massage was erotic and thrilling? Or did she tell him how watching him and Danielle make dinner melted her heart? Did she say how there was this stabbing ache when he drove away to catch the last ferry to the mainland?

Telling him felt cruel. "It was nice," she answered lamely. Doyle's eyebrows dropped down into what she called his dom stare and she squirmed beneath the look. "Really nice. Beyond nice."

"Do better."

Right. The truth. "He showed up when Danielle was having a tantrum over socks and it was such a relief to see him, Doyle. To know that I wasn't alone was so nice." The flinch around his mouth hurt her heart. She turned into a single mother when he was on tour, recording an album or even writing music with the guys. She had definitely raised their first daughter alone when he had been too out of it from his addictions. "It felt…normal. Like that was how normal people spent the day together," she continued in a quiet voice, hurting for her ex and for her too. She hadn't wanted to be married to Doyle Kole, bad ass drummer of the rock band Cyanide. She wanted to be married to Doyle Kolemann and sadly she hadn't realized they were one in the same until everything came crashing down. She had done him a disservice because she'd been unable to love all of the pieces of him.

"Sorry I couldn't give you that."

What could she say? "You tried, Doyle."

"I don't like to try. Trying feels like failing with an 'a for effort.' Enough about the past. Back to you and Oz and what brought you to my door tonight."

"I...I like him, Doyle," she whispered, meeting his eyes for the first time.

"What are we? Fourteen?"

"That's all I'm willing to tell you," she admitted. "What's a session lesson?"

Doyle blinked, reaching for his drink. "It's a punishment session before new members finish their orientation. If there are wronged parties they will be there, along with a few invited doms to initiate the new members. It's a way to teach the newbies that while kink is sexy fun, there's also a very real, very dangerous side to it."

"Dangerous?" That made sense. One of the first things she learned was that BDSM wasn't a game and there were serious consequences when something went wrong.

"If there are no punishments, depending on who's in the newbs, Oz will have a scene organized. Usually he runs it, but if it's an S&M crowd, Jensen will run the scene."

Holy shit. "What if it's a dom who broke one of the rules?"

"Since Oz won't strap another dom to the post, he

will use the dom's submissive or whomever was in the scene that went south."

"That's not fair. Not fair at all."

Doyle's grin crinkled the corners of his eyes. "You're cute in thinking fairness has anything to do with it. Consider what's said about a dom who lets a submissive be punished because they broke a rule? Nobody wants a bad reputation at Edge, honey. Nobody."

She nodded studied the pattern woven into the sleeve cuff of her sweater. "Do you hate me?"

He sighed. Reaching out, he gripped the back of her neck until she peeked up at him. "Nothing you do or have done in the past will make me hate you, Claire. You have done amazing things to keep our family together."

"Not everything was amazing, Doyle. I cheated on you."

He lowered his head so their foreheads touched. "We both know it's the only thing that would've made me go, even as it turned to ash around us. Was it a bad choice? You know it was because of how it makes you feel. But was it your only choice? Maybe it was. But I don't hate you. Not because of Jace. Not because of what is happening between you and Oz. Do you know why?"

She shook her head even as his beloved face blurred with tears.

"Because you deserve better than a broken-down addict with music in his blood and anger in his soul. You deserve someone to love you without limits."

"Doyle Kolemann, stop talking bad about yourself."

"You're not the boss of me, lady. Go be happy, honey. Go be the submissive you've always wanted to be but couldn't be with me because I was never here for you."

With a sigh, she wrapped her arms around his neck and held on. He was right. Sleeping with Jace Jennings was her one regret. She'd done it to hurt Doyle, to humiliate him. Because neither of them could end their marriage. Desperate times, she thought.

"Daddy, I have to pee." Danielle's voice came from upstairs.

Claire lifted a finger to her lips. The last thing their daughter needed was to find her there.

"I'll be right there, Dani."

When he went upstairs, Claire eased off the couch and shoved her feet into her rubber boots.

She *really* wanted to talk to Oz.

Oz – November 1989

He was pretty sure he heard Olivia wrong and she hadn't fucked Brock. Easing back, he looked down at her. Using her napkin, she wiped her eyes and began to talk without him saying a word.

"After you left Saturday, I did a scene with him. He cuffed me to the St. Andrew's cross and used a cane on me." Her face went soft and dreamy and Oz found himself shifting farther away from her. "He made Kerry kiss me from the other side. I've never kissed another girl. It was so…it was sexy, Oz. Soft to his hard strikes. I ached. Inside and out then he was inside me. Moving inside me. That hurt then it didn't – like when he beat me."

He really didn't want to hear how good it was for her to be fucked by another. She didn't even see him as she replayed the weekend. Because she spent the weekend with them, being topped by Brock, watching him top Kerry, the three of them fucking. Her cheeks were flushed, her pupils were blown out and her nipples were hard.

He withdrew his wallet and pulled a red fifty-dollar bill free, sliding it under his beer glass. "Good-bye, Olivia."

"What?" She blinked, returning to the present.

"You know where I stand with him fucking you."

"It's not like I meant it to happen, Oz."

"Yes, you did. You didn't have to scene with him because I wasn't there. Or maybe you did, but you didn't need to fuck him. Repeatedly. I get that you're impatient with me, but you don't know..." He stopped. She didn't want to know everything he had to take into consideration. "Good-bye." He stood up and walked away from her, Brock, and BDSM 101.

Chapter 12

FROM THE BALCONY of his condo, Oz looked out in the direction of where Claire was.

He was putting off a call he was pretty sure he needed to make and since the cordless was right beside him, he picked it up and called the familiar number.

"You're distracting me from important work," Jensen Evers said in way of a greeting.

"No, I'm not."

"I am a very important person, so yes."

Rolling his eyes, he turned his back on the view and stared into his condo. "Are you available tomorrow?"

"For?"

"Planning a S&M night at the club." He was taking Claire's uncertain maybe as a yes for now. If she changed her mind, members would still have a night. Maybe it was time to work it in permanently. Every once in a while, he thought of a permanent pain night, but he always talked himself out of it.

"I have the new girl coming tomorrow. We can tie her to the rafters and treat her like a piñata. We'll beat her until orgasms rain from her."

The scary thing was that Jensen meant it. Oz had no

doubt that when he arrived at Jensen's getaway, she'd be strung up in some diabolical way. "How's she working out?"

"She's relatively new, but fuck she can take a beating. And a fucking. Bring your mean tomorrow," the sadist said before hanging up. He wasn't one for long conversations.

Oz wandered inside and tossed his phone on the couch, sinking down beside it. Thursday seemed a long way away. He just had to do things his way.

He was pretty sure this was the longest three weeks in the history of the world. It was crazy how much he wanted to find the fastest way to get to where she was. How the hell had this happened?

Clasping his hands on the top of his head, he stared at the piano and then back at the phone. Impulsively he reached for the handset and dialed Claire's number. Was it too late to phone?

He felt like a nervous teenager phoning the cute girl at school he liked. This was ridiculous. He was a grown man and it wasn't even the first time he called her.

"Hello?" Her voice was breathless and while he could imagine her doing all kinds of naughty things to sound that way, he assumed she'd run for the phone.

"Hello, pretty girl. How are you?"

"Oz," she said in a soft tone. "I was going to call you."

"Were you?" It was ridiculous how much he liked knowing that. Unable to remain sitting, he stood up and wandered around his condo, avoiding the very prominent position of the piano.

"Yes. I talked to Doyle tonight."

He stopped walking, sitting at the breakfast bar so

his full attention was on her. "How are you?"

"Okay," she answered though she didn't sound entirely okay. "I feel – is it weird to feel relieved?"

"No. What did you tell him?"

"I told him about Jace. And you. I told him about you."

Shit. He needed to move again. "Me?"

"You. I told him you visited on the weekend. I told him how happy I was when you suddenly appeared like magic in the middle of Dani's tantrum because it was so nice to not have to be alone in that moment."

"I didn't do anything, Claire."

"You were here. Do you know how lonely it is to raise two little girls on my own? I know Doyle loves them but sometimes he's gone for so long and it's just me. It's easy to get overwhelmed, to feel like you're drowning when things are skewed. You think you did nothing with dropping by, cuddling me after, but it wasn't nothing, Oz. Not to me."

He rubbed a hand over his chest where his heart ached for her. She was killing him. How shitty did that make him feel that he never wondered how she was doing when she and Doyle were married and his friend was on tour? What a selfish bastard. "I'm sorry."

"For what?"

"Not realizing you went through this when Doyle was on tour. And with babies! Jesus, Claire."

"I had my friends for support, Oz. It wasn't your job to babysit your friend's wife and daughters. That's not what I said. I don't need your guilt for that, okay?"

Fair enough. "How is Doyle?" Meaning was the big bastard going to show up at his door and shove a drumstick up his ass before beating the shit out of him.

"Surprisingly he seemed fine."

"Really?" He doubted that.

"He says he's in no position to judge my life or choices."

Uh-huh. The big bastard was totally going to show up at his door. "Surprisingly fine" meant that maybe he'd get a warning before the beat down. Walking over to the floor to window, he gazed out at his view of Vancouver Harbour even though it was night and he saw nothing.

"What are you doing between now and Thursday?" He got to the point of the call. In the past, he had no problems separating himself from a session lesson. He also had no difficulties in implementing protocol when he was punishing a submissive. Again – something else he hadn't done with Claire. Because here he was.

"Uhm, worrying about Thursday."

He should really reassure her about session lesson and what he expected. But not yet. Where was the fun in reassuring her ahead of schedule? "Do you want to take a road trip? Tomorrow I'm going to go see Jensen. We have some things to discuss and the man hates using the phone. It's a long drive to his place because the guy lives in the middle of nowhere. Artists. We'll leave tomorrow, stay overnight before coming back. I'd say two nights but I don't want to rush Thursday."

She was quiet and he found himself folding his arm over his chest defensively. Once he noticed, he forced himself to relax. Jesus, man, how old are you? He sure as shit didn't feel thirty-nine during this conversation.

"I'd like that."

He smiled. "Me too. Pack one of your favorite little

sexy costumes. We'll undoubtedly play. I'm taking the first ferry over. I'd offer to do some island hopping to pick you up, but I really want to be on the highway early."

"That's okay. I'll meet you at the Victoria terminal. Am I bringing stuff for Thursday and Friday too?"

"Yes. So bring your second favorite too."

"I can do that."

He really wanted to play with her on the phone. "What are you wearing? Scratch that. What are you not going to be wearing in the next few minutes?"

The tiny catch in her breathing made him smile. "Everything?"

"Everything. Strip for me, sweetheart."

Claire couldn't remember the last time she packed for a trip anywhere. For some reason, she thought it was probably the last family vacation before Danielle was born. A rare event because Doyle hated going on holidays and being recognized. He preferred to spend time at home. While she understood, he didn't seem to understand that's the only place she really spent her time so vacations were a welcome treat.

Now she was away for the rest of the week. Sure, some of that time was just across the water in Vancouver. That wasn't the point. The point was that she didn't have to do anything. Unless Oz told her.

A shiver of delight moved up her back as she sipped her coffee, waiting for Oz. The entire trip from her home to here left her feeling nervous and anxious. Giddy. She was giddy as hell.

Hands rested on her shoulders and she tipped her head back to see Oz gazing down at her. God, he was so sexy he made her breath catch. Wearing his wool coat with a simple white tee beneath, he looked casual and comfy, with a dash of extra thrown in. It was that little extra something that made her stomach flutter and her pussy contract in memory of their phone call last night.

His hands slid under her opened jacket. He leaned down and kissed her slowly. His hands cupped her breasts, uncaring of anyone watching. Her nipples tightened as his fingers squeezed, his tongue dipping into her parted mouth when she gasped. Fingers pinched and caressed, their tongues meeting in slow, deep glides.

"Good morning, sunshine. Did you come last night?"

"No," she answered quietly, arching into his squeezing hands.

"This morning?"

"No."

His smile was slow and so wicked her thighs tightened. "Good." His hands slid free and she missed him touching her. He grabbed the handle of her suitcase and held out his free hand. Setting hers in it, she rose from her chair and followed him. He stopped at the ladies' washroom and handed her a small bag. "Swap out your panties."

Her heart began to race as she looked into his eyes. It wasn't hard to see the order, to see this man was in utter control of everything, including her. Especially her.

Her "yes, Sir" was automatic. In the bathroom stall, she discovered a round silver egg resting on a bed of yellow tissue. Wow. Okay.

Wow.

She dressed for road trip comfort. It took some careful manipulating of her yoga pants and ankle boots so she wasn't standing on the bathroom floor to remove her panties. The small vibrator easily slipped in, her pussy already wet from his kiss and the knowledge that they were in the beginning stages of a scene.

Wow. Okay.

Wow.

Getting back into her pants was as complicated as getting out. She had just pulled the waist over her hips when the vibrator began to shake and hum inside her. "Fuck," she gasped, a hand flattening on the stall wall. It quivered away, tickling sensitive tissue as she sat on the toilet to slip on her boots. The speed revved up and she panted as the wicked man outside woke up her body. The fabric of the black pants grew damp and she could only sit there, trying not to whimper as the vibrator teased and tormented her.

Oh god. Oh god!

She pushed the waistband down her thighs as the evil dom upped the wattage. She was going to come. In the women's washroom. One hand gripped her breast and the other curled into the toilet paper holder as the vibrator knocked repeatedly against her g-spot. She clapped her hand over her mouth to muffle any noise she made as it felt like Oz put it to the highest speed. The orgasm he'd denied her last night had chased her through dreams and this morning's shower hit her. Heat and need spilled through her and nothing was able to quiet the sound she made as she came.

Diabolical bastard. As if he knew, the speed abruptly shut off, leaving her gasping for air and her vagina quivering from the intense release. Leaning forward, she fought to catch her breath. She grabbed toilet paper to clean up the slick mess before pulling up her pants.

Her hands shook as she retrieved the small gift bag that now held her panties and her purse dangling on the door hook. She barely remembered to flush and wash her hands.

Oz leaned against the wall and glanced at his watch, giving her a mock scowl. "That took too long."

"You're an asshole," she muttered, holding out the bag. He looked in and gave a chuckle.

"It's a long drive, baby. I'd retract that statement or you'll find out just what kind of an asshole I can be."

"You made me orgasm."

"And without permission." He shook his head as he rested his hand on the small of her back. "I don't know what to do with that."

"Liar."

He grinned. "You're feisty this morning. I like it."

Somehow she had a feeling she wasn't going to like it. After all she was the one with a remote-controlled vibrator in her pussy and he held the remote. At his car, he popped the trunk and slid her suitcase in beside a black, ominous-looking duffle bag. Her stomach quivered. Every good little sub knew when her dom was lugging around his kit.

And she was a good little sub.

Oz – December 1989

"Hey Oz, someone here to see you."

Marking his page in his textbook, Oz left his dorm room to head downstairs. With exams beginning next week, the entire building was in a heightened sense of panic. Even his party roommates were cracking the books.

He was fairly certain it wasn't Olivia. Since their first and last date, he rarely saw her around campus. For the first time in his life, he was grateful for exams. They gave him something to focus on. He was able to forgive her a lot: the scenes with Brock, even the anal sex. It was the lack of respect he couldn't tolerate. Not even towards him, but to the kink. From the beginning he was taught that the safe word was pivotal and trust was golden. To say she hadn't meant to fuck Brock made a mockery of everything. And yes, she'd hurt him by not considering his needs at all. Both Olivia and Brock blatantly ignored his edicts about no fucking. Why was that request unworthy of either of them acknowledging it? Because he was new?

Fuck them both.

Pushing open the front door of his dorm, he was somewhat surprised to see the man sitting on the bench. His booted feet were crossed at the ankles while some cute girl flirted shamelessly with him. She didn't see the salt and pepper hair of a man at least twenty years older. He chatted with her, his aviator sunglasses reflecting her face back at her, his attention focused entirely on her. Her cheeks were flushed and not because it was winter. She absently fiddled with her hair in the way that said she was attracted and not entirely sure what to do.

Jamie reached into the pocket of his wool coat and held out a small book with a pen. Oz watched her eyes go wide. She found a page and wrote her number down. The older man took the book back and made a note. "Thank you, love. I'll call you over the winter break."

"Really?" Her eyes went wide.

He leaned forward and drew his sunglasses down, revealing his eyes for the first time to her. Oz swore he saw her panties get wet and she gave a shy smile. She gave Oz a double take as if realizing they weren't alone, and with a nervous wave to Jamie, she continued on her way.

"Seriously?" Oz stared at the dom who slid his glasses into place.

"Walk with me."

"Are you going to phone her?" Oz took the small book Jamie held out. He found the page where she wrote her name and number. Beneath it in neat print was *shy, potential pain slut - 12/22/89*. He had underlined the date and her name twice. "How can you tell?"

"She has scars on her forearm. I saw them when she was fiddling with her hair. I heard what happened with your girl."

"She's not my girl anymore."

Jamie nodded as he took the book back, returning to his pocket. "I would've come sooner, but I was out of town."

"Pretty girls to beat on?"

Jamie grinned and it made his face welcoming. "Sadly, no pretty girls." He patted his pocket. "Yet. I'd introduce her but I'm fairly certain the last thing you need is another kink virgin. Plus, I don't share. I'll partake with the willing, but I keep my pretty girls for myself. I assume you won't be returning to Brock's."

"You're very astute." Oz wondered why the man was here.

"Yes. It's also safe to assume you're in need of a mentor still. You haven't quite gotten your sea legs."

"Are you volunteering?"

"Good god, no."

Oz didn't know why the man's response reassured him, but it did. While he didn't know Jamie that well and the man had been helpful, he didn't feel like a good fit. Had Brock been? Or had he been his first and only choice? If Oz had met Jamie first would things have ended differently?

As they walked through the campus grounds, Jamie retrieved his notebook, and flipped to a page, tearing it out. "These are some recommendations for you. Find the right teacher for you," he said echoing Oz's thoughts. "And this is also for you." He handed him a second piece of paper and when Oz looked down he saw Dayna's name with her number.

His eyebrows rose as he faced it towards Jamie.

"She asked about you, asked if I'd pass along her number. She's a bratty sub, but she'd be good to learn on. She's been an active submissive for about eight years now and she's not afraid of a baby dom, her words. She's not looking for a boyfriend or a lover as she has a fiancé, but a dom is different than those. Between a good mentor and a seasoned sub, they'll get you on the right path. Brock was not the right choice for you, though I guess you learned some lessons, eh?"

Yeah, like never get a mentor who wanted to fuck your submissive.

Oz considered the list of names of potential mentors. There was even a female domme and he was intrigued by that. "Thank you. I'll phone them after winter break. I'm heading home for Christmas."

"Where's home?"

"Victoria."

Jamie tapped Dayna's number. "She's in Duncan."

Interesting. Oz slipped the papers into his pockets. "Why are you really here?"

Jamie gazed around, looking at Oz. "I dislike waste. Good luck with your exams and Happy Christmas, Oscar."

"Merry Christmas, Jamie. And thank you." He watched the older man walk away and pulled out the papers. He stared at Dayna's name. *Not looking for a boyfriend.* The phrase wandered around his mind as he walked back to his dorm.

For all his declaring not to be Oz's mentor, it seemed like the older dom was always teaching a lesson. Like dom didn't equal boyfriend. It was something Kerry and Brock had tried to teach him. Their final lesson had been brutal.

Chapter 13

SHE HADN'T MEANT to fall asleep on Oz thirty minutes in, but she warned him that car trips put her to sleep. Her dreams changed and blended as dreams did. They were in the middle of the pit at Edge. Just the two of them but they weren't alone. Nameless, faceless shadows watched as Oz snapped and tapped a cane over her naked body. She was naked on a round pedestal, her arms tied in intricate webbed rope behind her back, her thighs tied open as a penis shaped vibrator hummed in her pussy and a dildo filled her ass. The gag she wore wasn't a ball like when she had been at his condo but one phallus-shaped that she licked and sucked. Her eyes were covered so she couldn't see anyone, not even her dom, but she felt him all around her, even inside her where the sex toys made her ache to be filled by them. It was their phone call from last night.

The pain melded with her arousal, her body straining for the orgasm he kept her on the brink of. Every time he struck her, she mentally begged him to finally fuck her, to make her his.

"Tell me what you want," he whispered against her ear, bouncing the evil cane against one swollen nipple, his arm crossed over her front.

Yours. Make me yours.

"But you already are," his said. "Tell me what you want."

Fuck me and make me yours.

"You are already mine. Tell me what you *want*."

Everything. She wanted everything: the quiet Sundays, the erotic phone calls, the knowledge…the proof that she belonged to him, even this sweet pain. He resumed the strikes of the cane, hitting a little harder each time he walked around her. It hurt. So much.

Her orgasm was welcome until her eyes opened and she realized she really was climaxing from the bullet buried in her. Gasping for air, she looked over at the man who sat with his back against the door, his gaze on her and the remote in his hand.

Were they there?

A look out the windshield showed they were stopped alongside a road in the middle of nowhere.

Claire lowered her hand to her groin where the vibrator continued to quiver inside her. He lifted his hand and gave a crook of his finger. Unable to resist, she crawled over the console between them as he shifted his body. He helped her straddle his lap, her body still trembling from the dream and orgasm. She sucked in her breath to feel his erection press against where she was wet and aching.

She clutched his chest when his hands slid under the waistband of her pants and cupped her ass, rocking her over him.

"Take me out," he ordered, his voice low and rich with arousal and command.

Her fingers shook as they slid down his stomach to

the fly of his jeans. She couldn't look away from his eyes – the heat and promise in them made her stomach flutter. His nostrils flared when her fingers wrapped around the silky hardness of him.

"I could be balls deep in you right now," he said as she began to stroke him time to his hands working her. "I should be inside you."

"Yes," she whispered.

"Do you know why I'm not?"

Licking her lips, she nodded.

The seat tipped backwards behind him and he drew her shirt up. He didn't strip it off her but he hooked the neck over the back of her neck. Reaching to unclip her bra, he pushed the cups beyond the cotton that cupped her breasts. She cried out as he pinched her nipples.

A part of her couldn't believe they were doing this along the side of a road. Anyone could see them. She watched his eyes flick to the side mirror and back to her. That's when she realized if any vehicle came towards them, he would see.

"Use those hands of yours and make me come all over this soft skin." His hands slid back in her pants where he squeezed her ass. "Do you come?"

"No, Sir."

"Tell me your dream."

As her hands learned the shape of him, she did. Telling him her dream would've been sexy, and touching him added another dimension. When a finger caressed along the valley of her ass, she cried out, her fingers tightening in a way that made him moan. She loved that she was the one to draw that sound from him.

"Fuck, but I want to be inside you."

"Yes," she whispered, her hand sliding up and down as she lost herself in this moment. "Please. Please come on me."

"Jesus." His hand covered hers, tightening her grip so they were both working him. His eyes closed and he arched up with a guttural curse filling his car. She shivered as she felt the warm, silky splash of him coming on her stomach. His hand fisted in her hair, jerking her down to kiss her.

She may have been on top but he was utterly in control.

He eased her back onto his lap so she was leaning against the steering wheel. She gazed down at her stomach as he tucked himself away. She jumped when his hand suddenly went down the front of her pants. Feeling his fingers inside her made her cry out and arch, her hips bucking. Oh no, she thought. As he tugged on the toy, she fought her orgasm. But the feel of him drying on her skin, his fingers moving in her, was too much.

"Oh Claire," he murmured, "that wasn't well done at all." Once his seat was upright, he shifted her trembling body to her seat while he dropped the toy into the gift bag it had arrived in. "You can stay like that until we get to Jensen's."

"I think I hate you."

He grinned at her as he buckled her seatbelt. "Baby, we've just started. It's a long ride to the cabin. Glove compartment."

Oh. Oh no. With shaking hands, she opened it up and removed another gift bag identical to the first one. When she looked inside, she whimpered. Resting on bright yellow tissue were two of the most evil-looking nipple clamps she had ever seen. He plucked them free. Baring one breast, he captured a nipple in a painful pinch then the other. "So pretty," he said. He pressed a kiss between her breasts, slipping her t-shirt back into place. "Let me know when they start to hurt."

She nodded as he threw the car into gear and continued on.

Best road trip.

Ever.

She didn't know Jensen Evers that well. She was more familiar with his art, even before seeing the two at Oz's place. Jensen's art was blatantly erotic and unapologetically kinky. She knew he was a serious sadist who had intimidated her the few times she met him. When the gravel road they were on for what felt like the longest time finally spat them out into a coastal town, she was charmed. The Pacific Ocean was beautiful and the town adorably quaint.

"Jensen's family has owned the land for a few generations. When his grandparents died he inherited the cabin and his brother got the house in Victoria," Oz said, driving along what felt like a private road. A large intricate gate barricaded the road and a fence disappeared into the woods. "He takes his privacy very seriously." Instead of pressing the button on the box, he pushed down on the horn until the gate opened.

The gravel road meandered through trees until out of nowhere a massive house appeared. Cabin, she mentally snorted. Uh-huh. It was a beautiful two-storey log building with windows everywhere.

Oz parked beside a white compact car, turned off the

engine and held up a finger. She waited as he slid free, walked around and opened her door. He helped her out and she could only take in the quiet.

"On your knees."

She sank down to the cool, damp grass. He rested his hand on her head to keep her looking down, then opened the back door. Another bag identical to the previous gift bags was set before her and she stared at it, wondering what piece of torture waited for her.

"I debated about having you naked but I know how much you enjoy dressing up, plus the weather isn't conducive to nudity. From your suitcase, pick which outfit you want to wear. You can change out here. The only ones who will see you are Jensen, his submissive and myself. After you can open your last gift bag."

She nodded and he opened the trunk, pulling out her suitcase and setting it down before her. She unzipped it and debated about which one to wear. She had packed more than her favorite two. She may have gone a little crazy with packing, eager to reclaim these pieces of herself.

She glanced at Oz who leaned against the other car, his arms folded casually over his chest as he watched her, his big bag of bad at his feet. Every inch that he aroused over the trip perked up. She drew her shirt over her head, the cotton rubbing nipples still tender from the clamps hours ago. She removed the cropped shirt that was a lot smaller now than before her last pregnancy. Somehow she didn't think he'd mind there was a bit more Claire beneath the shirt with *spank me* in red glitter over her breasts. Next she removed her boots and pants, pulling a red pair of ruffled panties out and drawing them up without standing.

"Adorable. And I most definitely will."

She smiled as she folded her clothes back into her luggage. Finally, she reached for the bag and pulled out a pair of simple flip flops. "You're pretty clever, aren't you?"

"I am. You keep that sass up and I'll gag you."

Yes and *please* she thought before her brain derailed. The collar was simple: black leather with a silver buckle and d-ring. Her fingers trembled as she reached in to touch it, her gaze darting to the dom who approached her. He lifted the collar from the yellow tissue and slid it around her throat, buckling it without breaking eye contact.

"Some things are going to happen here today and they may upset you. This is to remind you that you're mine no matter what you see."

She touched the ring, hooking her finger in it. "What am I going to see?"

"I've been invited to scene with Jensen and his new submissive. He's a hardcore sadist and she's probably just as masochistic. Everything that happens here is consensual, but I'll understand if you need to safe out of watching. All you need to do is quietly leave."

"Why am I here?"

Fingers gently stroked over her cheek. "Because I want you here. What you will witness is not what happens in the club on designated nights. Those are controlled scenes. This isn't for everyone."

She frowned as he stood. "But you're not a masochist."

"No. I'm not. I won't stay the entire scene. Everyone, even doms, have a hard limit, and Jensen's lifestyle isn't mine. That doesn't mean I don't like making pretty little subs scream and cry."

He carried their luggage around the large house. They walked up some stairs on a hill and along the bluff. The building looked round, every wall a massive window that was opened like a door. White curtains billowed from the breeze off the ocean. She walked into something out of a twisted dream.

In front of one open window was a massive X made out of steel and wood. It looked ominous compared to the cross at the club. Edge's was made of out rich wood and padded with leather, this one was, truthfully, a little scary looking.

Her feet locked to the floor as her gaze bounced to the rest of Jensen Evers's BDSM collection. Was that a cage? It looked like a cage. She was pretty sure that was a cage raised from the floor, the door opened in a threatening manner. Who had a cage? Seriously.

Hands rested on her hips as Oz stood behind her, holding her as she took in someone's private play room. The most she had seen before were the bolts in Oz's shower. This was next level. Fingers lightly brushed her stomach as she struggled to catch her breath while she looked around. She couldn't even see what was on the other side of the circle of cabinets in the middle of the space.

Her gaze landed on the massive bed. The posts and canopy frame were also steel. The naked woman tied at the foot was a juxtaposition of softness to the bed. She wasn't just tied. Black rope coiled around her neck then to her breasts until they swelled almost painfully. Her arms were stretched out, the black rope looking like webbing around her arms until it reached to the metal posts. Her thighs were equally tied, legs open as she knelt there. Not even the black ball gag in her mouth could muffle the sounds she made as the dom in paint-splattered jeans fucked her ass. One hand was fisted hard in her hair, pulling her head back.

It was terrifying to see.

Erotic to witness.

One swollen breast was gripped in a way that made her own breasts ache. Claire's nipples swelled in arousal even as sympathy rippled through her because that was not gentle. The other woman cried out, her ass pushing back into her dom.

Fingers caressed the under swell of her breasts that were barely hidden by her shirt and she gripped the side seams of Oz's jeans as they watched the darkly erotic scene before them. Whatever the dom did had to hurt as tears slid down the woman's cheeks, but the sounds of animal lust from her told Claire that she liked the pain. A lot.

Against her ruffled panties, Oz was hard. His cock pressing against her ass. She couldn't look away as he cupped her breasts, tweaking her swollen nipples until she was arching against him.

Jensen reached into his back pocket, and flicked his wrist. A lethally sharp blade appeared and he drew the tip up the woman's stomach the slid it between her breasts. The knife sliced through the coils of rope with ease. She screamed, her entire body straining against the ropes as blood rushed to her breasts. Holding the flat of the blade between her heaving breasts, the sadist continued to fuck her hard as she climaxed until he found his own release with a loud growl and a final thrust.

Oz released her breasts and pressed his hands on her shoulders until she melted down to her knees. She watched as he approached the couple. Oz cut the rope from her neck with safety shears he had picked up, and helped Jensen free her from her webbing. The woman would've collapsed to the bed if Jensen hadn't caught her and lowered her down, stretching out beside her as he caressed her back, talking quietly to her.

Claire's body couldn't quite settle; she watched the couple, unable to look away from the way the sub curled herself around Jensen. Her own heart was racing hard, her body humming at what she had walked in on.

She didn't know how long she knelt there, staring, while Oz gathered up the rope remnants and tossed them into an aluminum trash can. Jensen stirred first, rising up on his elbow as he gazed down at his submissive. Looking over his shoulder, he caught Claire staring. She felt a visceral response as he looked at her. A hot twist of "holy shit, this man was hot."

How had she never noticed that he was down-right gorgeous?

His black hair was short, his jaw covered in thick black whiskers. Tattoos ran down his arms and a wicked looking phoenix soared from a blood red rose on his back. She couldn't stop staring at him as he rolled away from his submissive and off the bed. His jeans were old and threadbare with all kinds of streaks of paint everywhere. Heavy combat boots made clomping sounds on the floor as he walked towards her.

No, men walked.

Jensen Evers prowled.

He didn't look like an artist. He was too large, too lethal to be a simple artist. Her ex-husband was big: not just tall but so heavily muscled one's first thought was "thug," not rock star. Jensen could've been related to him.

A finger hooked into her collar and he drew her up on her knees. His eyes were the iciest, lightest blue she had ever seen, his skin a rich copper color that spoke of mixed heritage of some kind beneath the ink and sheen of sweat. "Has Oz explained what will happen here?"

"Yes."

"You are welcome to watch or participate. You are not welcome to judge or interfere. Everything that happens here is consensual. If you want to play, we'll negotiate over what because we all know this is beyond what you do. You will not belittle my sub for what she likes or needs. You are a guest here and if you are told to leave, you will not be welcomed back, no matter that Oz is your dom. This is a place of respect. Can you agree to those terms?"

"Can I ask questions?"

"Questions keep you safe. Yes. Can you agree to my terms, Claire Kolemann?"

"Yes," she whispered weakly. She cleared her and tried again. "Yes, Sir."

"Welcome to the Roundhouse, Claire. Would you like a tour?"

She nodded.

Still holding onto her collar with one hand, with the other he traced the script over her breasts. Against the white cotton her nipples tightened. "I accept your request," he said, pinching one prominent tip hard enough that she whimpered even as the ruffled panties grew wet.

His wink was pure wicked promise. "I'm showing your sub around, Peters."

"Fair enough. Tell him the rules, sweetheart."

Her eyes went wide and she looked from Jensen to Oz who was sprawled across the width of the bed, playing with the other woman's pale blonde hair. She had rules? Oz hadn't mentioned any rules for today. The only ones she knew about were…oh.

"No fucking until Thursday. No coming inside me… anywhere inside me."

Oz winked at her and this one was more reassuring than Jensen's. "No scening yet either. She's barely dipped her toe into the waters that flow through here."

"Well then, come along, Claire Kolemann, and see my waters."

Exhaling softly, she stood when he pulled on the ring. He held onto the collar as he walked her to the left. Surprisingly, the cross was even more intimidating up close. It looked mean and cold, with holes running along the fronts of the arms. "How does this work?"

He tugged on the collar, pressing her against the center of the X. When he walked away, she peeked over her shoulder. Jensen walked through one of the openings of the inner circle and after opening a cupboard, he came back carrying four cuffs in one hand and something else in the other. Claire could only watch as one thick, padded cuff was wrapped around her wrist and the brass buckle clipped into place. He decorated her other wrist and ankles the same way. He stood against her back, so close she could feel the heat of his stomach against her back. He lifted her left hand up and through the matching ring, he slid a bolt into the through then connected the other side.

The metal was cool against her stomach and arms and as he locked her into place, and her heart began to race. She shivered when he caressed his fingers up her legs, over the frilly ruffles covering her hips and up her ribs.

When his hands slid beneath her top to cup her breasts, she shivered. The man was as solid as the cross in front of her. He slowly squeezed her breasts, her nipples swelling. He continued to tighten his grip until it moved from a squeeze to a hard clamp. She gasped at the pain, her body trying to recoil away but he held her in place as the pressure tightened and tightened.

"What's your safe word, Claire?"

"Sunshine," she gasped out.

"Good girl." Her nipples were clamped between strong fingers and he continued to squeeze. She began to pant, the pain spreading through her breasts. "Breathe, baby," he ordered. Her pants turned into pained gasps and she arched into his hands. Her head fell against his chest, the pressure like a boa constrictor. She swore she could feel his fingers digging inside her, the pain twisting into hurt.

"Sunshine," she whispered.

He let go and she cried out as blood returned to the tender spots his fingers had pushed into. A responding heat soaked her panties while she swore she felt her blood humming in her head. "Again?"

She nodded. When his fingers covered her throbbing breasts again, her response was immediate instead of gradual. It was like her breasts already knew the pain and her body recognized the rush. Against the cross her hands fisted, her hips using his body as a brace. She tried to escape the pain his fingers delivered. He clamped on her nipples and instantly her cry escaped as she arched into the hurt. Tighter and tighter until he suddenly let go. She gasped, pain and pleasure burning through her, her body not sure what to do, then he squeezed again.

Correction: her body definitely knew what to do.

She gasped as her orgasm spilled hotly from her.

"Are you ready to see how this works now?" He lightly brushed his fingers over her sore breasts, rubbing slow circles over her nipples that felt like they'd never relax. Against her frill-covered ass, his hard cock dug into her, reminding her of what she had seen when she had walked in.

She gave him the only answer she had. "Yes."

Oz – December 1989

He didn't intend to pull out Dayna's number after his last exam. Nor the next day. He studied her name and number so many times, he memorized the digits. "Fuck it," he muttered and rolled off his bed. The room was empty with his roommates celebrating the fact that exams were over until next term. First there was the dial tone before he entered the numbers. It wasn't until the phone was ringing that he doubted the wisdom of this.

"Hello?"

Fuuuuuuuck. "Can I speak to Dayna?"

"Speaking."

Double fuuuuuuuck. "This is Oz. Jamie gave me your number. We met at Brock's."

She was quiet for a few heart beats and he wondered if he had made a mistake. "Hi, Oz. I know who you are."

She sounded different than he remembered. Not so…in his face with her attitude. "I'm glad you called. How are you?"

Horny. Frustrated. Mad as fuck. "I have no idea what I'm doing, to be honest."

"Well, we already knew that." He heard the smile in her voice and he grunted in response. "You already know I'm a brat, Oz. Don't be surprised when I brat."

"I don't know how this works. What are we supposed to do?"

"How about we meet for drinks and talk."

He rubbed his hand over his head. "I thought you don't like interviews."

"So don't interview me. You're at UBC, right? How about we have drinks and talk. Let's meet at the Angelica, in say four and half hours, in the Garden. Will that work?"

"Jamie said you're in Duncan. That's a ways for you to go for drinks, Dayna."

"Four and half hours. If you don't show up, it's no problem. Just lose my number. I'll see you soon, Oz."

The Darling Hotel Angelica, was a posh building of glass, brick and limestone. Standing before it as his cab sped away, he couldn't ignore the beauty in the art deco design. The pristine lines were broken up by limestone carvings that pulled from the scenery of around Vancouver: ocean waves, the Rocky Mountains and even marine life. The entrance was a glorious masterpiece of glass, steel and copper. The building never failed to make his heart dance with joy when he came to study it.

Art Deco fascinated him. He liked the clean look of

it with the splashes of grandeur in carvings or roof decorations, as if the architecture was saying "yes, we rose out of the ashes of war, but we are glorious."

The doorman opened the door and Oz approached with none of his usual ease. He wasn't here to take in the architecture or art. He was here for drinks. With a submissive.

Jesus. What was he doing?

The hotel had three bars. There was a private one on the seventeenth floor, a masculine bar that made him think of smoking jackets and brandy, and one off the indoor garden that everyone simply called the Garden. He was early. Unable to remain in his dorm, he had finally called a cab. His nerves were jumping like they never had before.

After making sure Dayna hadn't arrived yet, he found a quiet booth and ordered a beer. He needed something to do with his hands or he'd run screaming from the hotel, never to return.

Folding his arms on the table, he looked out into the greenery beside him. During the day, it was loud and busy. Nighttime, there was a noise by-law as a few floors above the park hotel rooms surrounded the space. The interior rooms cost a freaking fortune and were hard to get. Reaching for his beer, he glanced around. Couples were scattered around, as were solitary travelers.

And then she walked in.

It took him a few minutes to recognize Dayna. Usually she was naked and sassy. This woman wore a tight pencil skirt that hugged her curves, high heels so high he had no idea how she walked but made her legs look amazing. The white blouse hugged her breasts and showed off the rich coffee color of her skin and her hair was both sleek and wavy. Jesus.

She was sex walking. He noticed more than one man turn to watch her hips swing with each step.

The smile she gave him was one of relief.

As she slid into the seat across from him, he couldn't help but remember that the first time he had seen her she had been naked, on her hands and knees as Brock's stool. Against the fly of his jeans, his cock swelled and he mentally lectured it that they weren't here to fuck or top or anything beyond drinks.

"Hi, welcome to the Garden. Can I get you a menu?"

"I'll have the house red," Dayna said, setting her small black purse on the table. "Thank you. Hi."

"Hi. I've never seen you in clothes before." Her dark eyes went wide and she gave a quick look to see if anyone cared about their conversation. They didn't. "You wear them beautifully. Though I'll be honest, at this moment you're a naked piece of furniture in my head."

Her lips parted in surprise and he mentally high-fived himself when her nipples swelled against her blouse. "Well…okay," she said. When her wine was set down, she took a sip. "Am I your furniture?"

"You're a table for my beer as I fuck you."

Beneath her blouse her breasts rose and fell. "And if your beer topples?"

He found himself smiling and her breath caught. "I stop fucking you."

"I have a room."

"I have a beer."

Making his way back to his dorm room, Oz felt like

he may not suck at this. Being with Dayna was vastly different than Olivia. He hadn't worried about the tiny details as they had played in the hotel room. She had brought her own little BDSM kit along and let him use everything she had packed. When he hadn't used the riding crop hard enough, she had let him know and when it was too hard, she had also been vocal about it. He had used her pink leather cuffs on her wrists and ankles, immobilizing her as she gave him a blow job that had ended with them fucking, her awkwardly bent over the chair he had been sitting in.

Had she been mouthy? Only until he had shoved a face cloth in to silence her.

It had been…fun. Friday nights were her night to submit. Her fiancé, who she clearly loved and let her have one night to satisfy the needs he couldn't, worked in computer software engineering and had to cross the border every week for a meeting. It gave her just enough time to scene before they'd meet at the Darling and head home.

There was no pressure. He didn't look at her kneeling and think she was fragile. He didn't worry about every lesson he'd learned; instead, it had been natural. Before he had left her waiting for her guy, they had talked because she had been really surprised that he hadn't sucked as much as he had at Brock's.

"He's not your friend," she had said as they cuddled. Her aftercare involved a lot of cuddling. "I know you know that now and it's a bitter lesson to have learned. Yeah, he's a helluva dom, but he's a dick. You were a welcome distraction from the regular Fridays. He mindfucked you into next year. You're new and I guess I forgot that. I gave you shit without seeing what was going on. What he and Kerry did to you was a massive fuck you. Do you know why I love being submissive?

"I like knowing I'm safe with whatever happens. I trust the dom to respect my needs and my limits. They didn't respect you or your limits because he wanted to fuck the virginal submissive half his age. New or seasoned, that's important. What I'm saying is I'm sorry. When you trust yourself, Oz, you are really good at this. So keep trusting yourself, and if you want, I'd like to do this again after Christmas."

The last thing she had said to him was to bring his bag and she'd wear a bow for him.

He felt amazing. Like he was high on life. He. Didn't. Suck.

"Dude," Aaron said the minute he walked into their room. "Your mom has been calling every hour. Hysterical."

Oz froze as he looked at his roommate. Hysterical was not a word he'd use on Vanessa Peters. "Why? What happened?"

"Your sister is in the hospital."

Chapter 14

"THESE ARE FUCKING adorable," Jensen said, his fingers fluffing her panties. "I bet Oz loves them. He says you're having thoughts of attending an S&M night and that's why he's here, to plan one." Fingers casually stroked up and down her hips, his denim soft against her skin. "What's your experience with pain?"

"Impact play with Doyle. Then, uhm, the night at Edge."

"Hm. Yes. You do that here and that's it, Claire."

"I know. It was…I was–I don't know. Looking for something." And wound up finding Oz. Crazy.

"What were you looking for? What do you want the pain to give you?" His caressing hands moved to her stomach.

Absolution. The word made her jolt. Hands flattened on her stomach, the arousing touch coming to a stop. The sadist kissed the crown of her head. They stood like that as the word made the back of her throat shrink.

"Do you know the definition of a masochist, girl?"

"Someone who likes pain. A lot."

His chuckle was soft, his fingers lightly strumming up and down her stomach. "It's someone who finds pleasure in pain. Do you know why pain is my kink? There's an honesty to it. You either like it or you hate it. You either want more or you want none."

She whimpered when his hands cupped her tender breasts. "Oh, I like that sound," he said against her ear. "I like turning it into something more. I'm going to leave your adorable fluff ball panties on. I'm going to strike this ass five times, each time progressively harder." He gave her bum a squeeze, and stepped away. "Despite the padding, it will hurt. Because I like to make it hurt. When it becomes too much, what's the word you use?"

"Sunshine."

"Good girl. Nothing I do will permanently mar you, Oscar was quite clear on that. Understand?"

She nodded, jumping when he pinched the back of her thigh hard enough to make her flinch. "Yes, Sir."

"God, subs are delicious."

He left her bound to his cross and she glanced over her shoulder at the bed. Oz met her gaze before rolling off the mattress and walking over to her.

Even though everything screamed at her that Jensen was a sexy beast, it was watching Oz walk that made her heart race faster. He stopped behind her and she shivered as his hands caressed her waist. When the sadist touched, he could turn her on, but this was different. This she felt all the way to the deepest corners of herself.

"You look tempting trapped here. Like a ruffled package for me to unwrap. He made you come. Your poor breasts have had a rough time today." He lightly massaged her breasts. She couldn't stop the tiny flinch when he stroked her nipples. "We've talked about this, Claire." There was an ominous tone to his voice. "You don't hurt yourself unnecessarily. What's the word?"

"Sunshine, and I know. They're just tender. I don't know what's worse, your clamps or his fingers."

Oz kissed the back of her neck. "Jensen is back. Are you ready?"

"Five strokes."

"You say that like you can take it." He slid around so he stood before her. Reaching up, he curled his hands around the bolts that held her in place.

"This is Lucifer. He's made of medical-grade steel. He likes ruffles." And the first hit came.

She wasn't sure what she had expected but it sure as hell wasn't the forceful blow that made her cry out. Had she not been pinned against the cross, she would've buckled.

"I can make you scream," the sadist said, "and beg for more. I can twist the sharpest pain into the sharpest pleasure. I can make your orgasm hurt. And what's more, I'll love every single moment of it. Imagine this but more. More pain until you swear blood is spilling from your body as I create a masterpiece of hurt. I can turn this cunt into a work of art beneath anything in the Roundhouse, including my knife. This," he pushed his hips into her tender ass and she hissed at the contact, "makes me want to wreck your body and put it back together."

Oz's eyes narrowed and he took a slow, deep breath. She did too, unable to look away from him. Something was stirring in him, but before she could ask, Jensen sent Lucifer crashing down again.

Mother-fucker! This was him starting off light? What would it be like by number five? Everything in her body was screaming *NonononoN-O*. There was impact play and then there was hell on earth that was Jensen. She didn't want to wimp out but holy God. Holy shit. What was radiating from her ass was not pleasant. Nothing about how her bum throbbed from the two blows was in any way, shape or form sexy. And Oz. His face was tight, his mouth a flat-line. He didn't like this. At all, but was allowing this for her. She could do this. Really.

"This is done," Oz said. The look on his face made her stomach tight.

"Jesus, girl," Jensen muttered behind her.

She barely heard him walk away, her attention locked on the man who crouched down and released her ankles from the cuffs. Her heart began to pound as Oz slowly rose up. He moved as if every inch up hurt his body. Her mouth went dry when he glanced at her, his eyes resembling hard chips of greenish-gold ice.

Reaching up, he gripped the top of the X and exhaled slowly. "Do you remember what I said would end this?"

She blinked and her racing heart gave a painful squeeze. "Yes," she whispered, her mouth suddenly desert dry.

"Tell me."

Swallowing, she fought to get the words out. "If I permitted harm by not using my safe word." Every word hurt more than her bum from the two brutal strokes from Jensen. "I'm sorry, Oz."

He reached down and released the pins and her arms dropped like hundred pound weights were wrapped around her wrists instead of simple leather cuffs. She felt cold as he looked at the cross, his eyes scanning it slowly before he finally looked at her. The pain on his face robbed her of breath.

"I can't do this, Claire. I *won't*. I'm done."

"No. Oz–"

He held up his hand to stop her and he walked away.

She turned to watch him approach the bed, grab his bag, and continue out of the roundhouse. Jensen studied her before following his friend out. Wait. No!

She ran to the door he had disappeared through, the winter chill nipping at her bare legs as the hill swallowed up Oz. "Oscar!"

Pants. She needed pants. Her suitcase waited for her by the bed, filled with sexy outfits she had brought for him. She found her yoga pants on top and she jerked them on and found the flip flops he had given her.

Running in them was difficult. Every time one fell off she had to slip it back on so the gravel of the path down to the house didn't cut into her feet. The damn shoes ate up valuable time so when she reached the yard, his car was already driving away. Jensen stood staring at the tail lights. "I'll take you home when you're ready."

"He left," she rasped out, pressing a hand over her heart. "He just…left."

"Everyone has demons, baby. Even the man who looks like he has none."

"But–"

"What's the word you thought of?"

"Absolution." Just saying the word made tears burn her eyes.

Beside her Jensen sighed. "There is no forgiveness in pain, girl. Not even the consensual kind. It will chew you up and it'll tear you apart. Pain isn't your truth. It isn't your beauty. So why permit it? That first hit told you exactly what to expect. Everything inside you cried out at you to stop. I saw it. Oz saw it. But you let the second strike happen. That's dangerous in this world, Claire. You know better. That's what started this. People can die in this. People *have*. You need to figure your shit out before something far worse happens than someone beating your ass with more force than you want or like. Daisy will bring your things down. Wait inside where it's warmer."

She felt numb as she walked up the stairs of the porch that wrapped around Jensen's home. He draped a blanket over her, tucking it around her so she was warm. Inside, she was freezing.

He had left. Not just left but left her. Exactly as he had warned her he would. Because she hadn't listened to herself.

Lifting her hands to her mouth, she used the blanket to muffle the sob that escaped.

Jensen's submissive entered wearing a pair of sweatpants and a hot pink fleece jacket. She set the suitcase down, coming over to hold Claire. This young woman, who was an utter stranger, held her as she cried.

The artist returned wearing a jacket while carrying a black hoodie. He eased the blanket free and slipped the large sweater on. "Come on, baby, let's get you home."

How? It was night. The ferries were closed and the drive to Victoria was long. *So long.*

She was led to a detached garage and he drew open the two doors. He helped her into the large SUV, tucking the blanket around her before snapping the seatbelt in place. Her suitcase was stowed in the back seat. As he drove, he pulled out his cell.

"Hey, it's Jensen. Sorry. Can you meet us at Montague in an hour? It's bad. I wouldn't let her be alone.

No." He was quiet. "No. Okay. Thanks. See you in a bit."

"Who was that?"

"Doyle. He's going to pick you up at the Galiano marina in an hour." He pulled into his town's marina. "Simon will be here in ten minutes. Do you want a coffee? Tea?"

"No." She wanted Oz. "Will he be okay on the road? It's dark."

"I'll call him in a few hours to make sure he made it."

"Will you let me know?"

He studied her and nodded. "I don't know you well, Claire, but I hope you'll take my advice on this. You need to figure out why you're doing this to yourself. Why would you keep a scene going when it feels wrong in every way?"

"I don't know," she whispered.

"Those are three really dangerous words. If I had a sub say that to me, there's no way I'd continue with her. You know this world. You're not new to it. You know trust is pivotal to this. You trust us to not hurt you, but we trust you to stop us when it does hurt or doesn't feel right. If you can't do that, maybe you shouldn't be doing this anymore. Oz has reasons why this is a hard limit for him. Good reasons. Hard taught reasons. The kind that are born from pain, not just because he loves kink. He respects this world, he respects those who submit because he knows how strong submissives truly are, and it's one of the reasons he built Edge. But if you can't trust...if he can't trust you to trust him then he's not going to do this anymore with you. There's Simon."

Tears fell, each word he said was like a nail into her heart. "Who's Simon?"

"Pilot. Let's get you home, baby."

Closing her eyes, she tried to block out the noisy float plane. Jensen was right. She *knew* better. After ten years in the kink world, five and half years married to a dom, she knew trust was the glue to a D/s relationship.

She trusted Oz. She truly did. Claire knew he'd never hurt her, but that wasn't the problem. The problem was she'd done the same thing with Jensen that she had done with the man at the club. The only difference between the two episodes was that this time she wasn't walking away covered in bruises. This time her heart was hurting.

Because she had hurt Oz.

More than once he had brought up the importance of using her safe word. He respected her hard limits, so why hadn't she respected his? Reaching up, she touched the collar Oz had put on her. What was wrong with her?

When she had gone to Edge almost a month ago, she hadn't gone intending for everything to go wrong. Loneliness was what had taken her to Edge. She missed the care and touch of a dominant. After the divorce, she had locked up key pieces of herself because finding someone so close after the end of her marriage felt wrong.

She hadn't expected to find a dom, especially not with Oz. So why hadn't she reacted to him as she had the forgotten man and Jensen?

That, she realized was another question to ask herself. But later. She needed to figure out *why* she had behaved as she had because the idea of Oz no longer in her life was devastating. She had nobody to blame but herself.

Resting her head on the window, she looked at the man in the co-pilot's seat. What had she been trying to prove to herself? Not just with Jensen but with the other dom? God, she wished she remembered his name. Every time she called him "that dom" or "the other dom" in her head, she felt shittier and shittier. She had originally wanted to prove that she could be with a dominant who wasn't Doyle, but that didn't explain Jensen. Because not only wasn't he her ex-husband, he wasn't Oz.

It was like she was punishing herself for dumb decisions. She couldn't even remember why she had agreed to that first scene. Because he had asked? Because he had been the instant cure-all for ending that loneliness? For feeding the starving submissive inside her? What a dumb reason to scene with someone. Because it had been a bad choice she had subconsciously decided to punish herself? Really?

So what was Jensen? Punishing herself for being curious about sadism when it wasn't what turned her on? Really?

No. That was stupid. Both reasons were…stupid.

And not true.

What had Jensen said? Oz needed to trust her to trust him. And she did. Wholeheartedly.

The one she didn't trust was herself. She had done the unspeakable to her husband. Even though they had talked about it, she had broken not just her vows to her husband but the vows to her dom.

And what had today been but another betrayal to her dom? Not just her breaking his hard rule of not using a safe word, but seeking something…more.

She wasn't a masochist. She knew that. Especially after a scene with a sadist who had barely done anything to her. So why had she been curious about more? What had she been trying to prove?

Why couldn't she be happy with what she had? Why couldn't she trust herself anymore?

It could not keep going back to how she had ended her marriage, because that was a lame excuse.

Her life was awesome. She had two beautiful daughters, her relationship with her ex was disturbingly positive and now there was this new relationship that was everything she had wanted her marriage to be.

Oh. Oh no.

Exhaling softly, she closed her eyes as that thought hit her where she lived. She had loved Doyle, but not enough. She had loved pieces of him and not the entire man, which was unfair to both of them.

With Oz everything was…everything. And what had she done? Exactly what she had done with the club dom *and* Doyle.

Foolish Claire, she thought. Foolish, stupid Claire.

She spotted Doyle when Jensen opened the door on the noisy float plane. Her ex-husband rose up from his crouched position like a giant emerging from stories. Jensen jumped down and went over to talk to him while Claire battled with her safety belt. The tears hadn't stopped falling the entire flight.

Finally free, she made her way over to the door, every muscle and joint hurting. Her sore ass hadn't liked the flight. At all. There was no one to blame but herself. Doyle approached and helped her out.

He cupped her chin in his hand and stared down at her. "You okay?"

Shaking her head, her "No" was quiet. He drew her

in, the leather of his jacket cold against her warm cheek. He sighed and kissed the top of her head. "I fucked up, Doyle."

"Yeah. Let's get you home." He kept an arm around her shoulders and held out his hand to Jensen. "Thanks, man. Let me know when you land."

"Will do." Jensen handed over her suitcase. "You think about what I said, yeah?" She nodded and he kissed her forehead before disappearing inside the plane. They didn't watch it ferry away from the dock then eventually take off from the water. Doyle walked her along the dock, each step making it move beneath them.

They didn't speak as he loaded her into his vehicle and drove to his house. She was surprised to see Heather looking concerned in the living room, there to watch the girls. Doyle guided her upstairs to his bathroom. "Take a shower and get some sleep. I'll be downstairs on the couch." Grateful that she wouldn't be alone, she stripped and stepped into the shower.

She had never been in here. Well, briefly when the house had first been built but she always respected Doyle's home and space. Turning the water as hot as she could tolerate it, she released the sobs that she swallowed down for the hour.

He had left and she knew it was her fault. She had broken him because something in her was broken.

Oz – December 1989

Her fair skin was colorless as she lay in the bed, the monitor quietly counting her heartbeats. The fairy princess resembled someone who had her wings ripped off.

Oz gently stroked each still finger as he gazed at his

sister. Never had getting to Victoria taken so long. Instead of the ferry, he had pulled out his credit card for emergencies and booked a very expensive thirty-minute flight and had a hired car waiting for him to bring him to the hospital. Never had he been more grateful for his father's money.

His mother was the one to find Kelsey collapsed at her beloved piano, pills scattered around her. No one knew where she found the sleeping pills because neither of his parents had prescriptions.

He had no idea what would drive his big sister to swallow pill after pill. Everyone was a little mystified. And worried.

So very worried.

His mother was hysterical, sobbing against his father when Oz had arrived. They pumped her stomach and now she was sleeping. What happened when she woke up? Did psychologists come or was that only in the movies?

"Fuck, Kels," he murmured. He leaned forward and rested his head on the bed, lifting her elegant fingers to rest on his head. When they were kids, she would use his head as a piano, lightly tapping out a melody. The stillness of her fingers terrified him. For a non-religious person, he found himself praying that his sister would open her eyes and would come back to him. He'd fix whatever had driven her to the pills.

He'd come home more often, talk to her more.

It was his job to look out for his sister so he'd do whatever it took to help and protect her.

"Ozzie?"

Her voice, thin though it was, made his entire body

shake with relief. "Hey Maestro."

"Where am I?"

"Hospital." He raised his head and caught her hand in his. He saw the confusion in her eyes as she looked around the room.

"But– How'd I get here?"

"Mom found you at the piano. Do you remember what happened?"

She nodded and shut her eyes. "The music. It hates me now. Can you go away?" She eased onto her side, her back to him.

"No." He climbed onto the narrow hospital bed and lay behind her. "It's okay, Kelsey," he said quietly. She began to cry. Hard, heartbreaking sobs that were probably hell on her traumatized body. He began to hum. Oz didn't have her skill with music so it was the first song that came to mind, which was Brahms' Lullaby. When her sobs quieted, he stopped abusing the song. He knew she still cried from the way she sniffled. "Music doesn't hate you."

"Yes, it does. If it liked me, it would let me play it."

"Remember what I said about you riding your bike?"

She snorted. "This is easier, Ozzie. Or it used to be."

"The mountains aren't ugly because of the climb. Music is the same way. You're still climbing the mountain, Kelsey. Do you know how sad the world would be without you playing your music? No one would send me Beethoven. And that breaks my heart."

"But I can't play, Ozzie. If I can't play, what's the point of me being here?"

Jesus, that logic ripped through him. "One note at a time, big sister. We do it one note at a time." Closing his eyes, he hugged her, afraid to let her go. The world would be a dour place without Kelsey Peters in it. *His* world would be a nightmare.

"One note," she whispered.

"We can do one note at a time. Okay?"

She nodded and he shuddered. His mind throwing what ifs at him faster than she could learn an instrument. What if his mother hadn't gone to check on Kelsey? What if he hadn't made it here in time? What if she had been all alone?

What ifs were the creations of nightmares.

Arms folded over his chest, Oz stared at where his sister was found. For the first time in years, the grand piano was silent. It looked abandoned without it's devotee. The black wood gleamed in the sun, the music that was stressing out his sister so much was still in place.

He wanted to set it all on fire.

"Oscar, honey," his mother's voice interrupted and he looked over his shoulder. Kelsey's suicide attempt had aged his mother. Her blonde hair seemed faded in its blunt bob, her blue eyes haunted. This had terrified her. "There are some police officers here to see you." She looked scared as she fussed with her hair.

He caught her hand and squeezed it. "Go lie down, Mom." She blinked at the name. She had always been Mother to him, but Kelsey had scared him too. Fear and love and awe at her had changed her back to Mom. Vanessa Peters had become a mama bear. Her child was in danger and she wanted to know what was next. She was on top of everything; at the hospital, she had asked questions about tests, talked to the psychologist. She even fired Kelsey's piano teacher, which Oz thought was amazing.

Christmas had been somber, even though Kelsey came home on the twenty-third. His sister was struggling and had yet to play the piano. She hadn't even wanted to hear Christmas music. He was *very* worried about his big sister.

"Do you need me?"

"I'm okay, Mom." He wasn't. School started tomorrow and he had made zero plans to return. His father was disappointed in him, disappointed in Kelsey. Oz thought his father could go fuck himself but he kept that to himself.

"Are you sure?"

"Positive." He left her to head up to her bedroom, knowing she'd look in on Kelsey, who was sleeping. Curious as to why the police were here, he went to the front room. Two cops in uniform looked very out of place in the feminine room. "I'm Oscar." He held out his hand, surprising the younger cop.

"You're a hard man to find, Mr. Peters."

"Not really. I've been here since the seventeenth when my sister was in the hospital." The two men looked at each other. The older reminded him of the older cop from the Lethal Weapon movies. His dark hair was greying and his face wore a few miles. He looked at Oz with a wary kindness.

"Do you know Olivia Swallow?"

His heart began to pound at her name and he had visions of them slapping handcuffs on him, hauling him away for abuse. "We dated for a month." Was that it? Saying it out loud made him pause. Wow, it felt so much longer. "I last saw her on October tenth."

The cop wrote in his notebook and Oz stared at it hard. "Are you sure of the date?"

"Pretty sure since that's when we broke up." He couldn't remember the date they met but the tenth was ingrained on his brain.

"What were the circumstances of your break up?"

"She slept with someone else." He hated saying the words, hated what they meant.

"Can you tell us who?"

"Can I ask what this is about?" They didn't answer, they just looked at him and he suddenly wished his mother was here. Maybe a lawyer or two.

They were waiting for a name and he really didn't want to because there would be questions and speculations: how had they met? Wasn't Brock Avery married?

Why was he protecting any of them? He exhaled slowly as he worked through this quagmire. Fuck. "Brock Avery," he muttered and watched both cops blink.

"Related to Joshua Avery who is also your roommate. When is the last time you saw Joshua?"

He had no idea. They weren't friends. During exams, but as he reminded them he'd been here since the seventeenth.

"If you hear from Joshua Avery, we'd appreciate you contacting us." They handed him a business card.

"I probably won't see him until I'm back on campus. We're not friends or even friendly. Seriously, what's going on?"

"Unfortunately, Miss Swallow passed away and we can't go into details. Thank you for your time, Mr. Peters."

Oz stared at the card. "What? She's dead? How?

What..."
Olivia.

Chapter 15

"ISN'T THERE A rule about drinking alone?"

The voice surprised him and Oz tilted his head back on his chair to see the woman walk through the bar. The smile that appeared was automatic. "Hello, beautiful, are you lost?" Dayna Reeves looked as if she had just walked out of a meeting. Maybe she had.

Approaching fifty, no one would guess. Her dark hair was glossy as it hung past her shoulders, her body still looking good even after two kids. She dropped down on his lap and gave him a long kiss. She sighed happily and cuddled against him. Even though they hadn't lasted long as dom and sub, they remained good friends. He had gifted her with a lifetime membership at the club when he opened, but she had never used it and likely never would.

When he had first met her she had been engaged to a man who wasn't a dom. Nice guy. It should've been weird to meet his submissive's fiancé, but it hadn't. A month before their wedding, a car accident on his commute to Seattle ended in tragedy and a week later Dayna learned she was pregnant. It was their mutual friend Jamie Hennessey who introduced Dayna to the man who became her dom and then husband.

Resting his hand on the curve of her hip, he watched her take his drink. "What brings you here?"

"You. Jensen phoned me."

"Ah," he said and lowered his head again. "I'm fine."

"You're so full of shit. Tell me about this girl."

"She's Doyle's ex-wife."

She whistled. "Tricky. But that's not who she is, that's what she is. Who is this submissive who finally snagged Oscar Peters' attention in a way that has him drinking alone in his club?"

"She's sweet. Sexy. I topped her by accident after a bad scene. She didn't end it…wouldn't. It was bad, Day. But I couldn't…can't get her out of my head. She crept inside me when I wasn't looking."

Dayna rubbed his chest. "So what ended it?"

"Jensen topped her and it wasn't what she wanted, but she wouldn't end it. I can't go through that again, Day," he said quietly.

"She reminds you of Olivia, doesn't she?"

Wincing, he took his glass back. "In some ways, not in others."

"Tell me what ways?"

"Her sweetness, the pure core of her, her joy in submitting. But twice now a scene went bad because she wasn't willing to stop it."

Dayna eased off his lap, settling into a chair beside him. She propped her feet on his thighs and he eased off her high heels and began to rub her toes. "Do you know why? Does she? You're a good dom, Oscar." She poked him. "I get that this triggered you, but we had scenes that didn't go right and you didn't walk away. We ended because we weren't the right person for each other. I'm a bratty sub and that irks the fuck out you. Even before we were together, I bugged the crap out of you. You said she got inside you and that's probably what hit the switch for you. I've been a bottom for Jensen. I vowed to myself that I could handle whatever he dished out. That fucker is hard core. I thought that I could take it. How bad could it be? I told Caleb it was the first time I'd ever safed out of a spanking scene with a riding crop. Caleb laughed because he knows just what this ass of mine can take. It cannot take Jensen Evers, no matter what I told myself. Could be she thought she could take it too. Ahh, that spot. Nice."

Oz shrugged. "I still can't be with someone who ignores limits, Dayna. Whether they're mine or hers. It's how people get hurt."

Dayna pulled her foot back and leaned towards him, her dark eyes looking both soft and fierce. "Olivia didn't die because she ignored her limitations or yours. She died because she made the dumb decision to scene with someone who had no idea what he was doing. Zero idea. You were new, yeah, but you knew what to do: how to make a scene safe, how to tie ropes, where to knot them, where not to place them, and how to look for danger signs. Olivia fucked up that boy's life, and her own, because she needed the high of subspace more than she needed a dom. Yeah, in the group she had a bad reputation, but if she asked anyone, they would've found a dom for her. Hell, had she asked you, you'd have asked Jamie or me if we knew anyone for her. She made the decision to have that poor kid tie her up in his dad's house to the cross with zero instruction on how to do so. He didn't know anything. And she didn't know anything because she left it to you to learn everything. That's what makes you a good dom, Oz. You listen, you learn, you pay attention. This scene with Jensen was nothing like Olivia. Nothing. Does she know about her?"

He winced and looked at the club he had built because of why Olivia died. Zero instruction and a lot of dumb choices from lack of options. "No."

"She needs to know, Oz. She should've known the minute you laid down the rule of what happens when you don't use a safe word when she's your sub. I didn't need that talk because I knew Olivia, selfish twat that she was. Not once in all the years I've known you has any sub gotten under your skin, as you said." She tapped her finger on the table, making her point. "No one lasted beyond a scene or two because you're you. You don't play at being a dom. All you've ever wanted was a sub of your own. Well…you have one and you're fucking up. I love you, Oscar, I really do, but if you don't chase her, I'm taking back the title of godfather to my boys."

Oz reached out and ran his knuckle down her cheek. "They love me and wouldn't stand for that."

She snorted. Rising up from her chair, Dayna gave him another kiss. "Answer me this, Sir, is this the submissive for you? Is she the one you want?"

He had only one answer. The truth. "Yes."

"Then fucking go get her. Olivia wasn't your fault. She was never your fault. You ending this relationship because this woman hit your trigger, *that's* your fault. When you've fixed this, bring her to dinner. We'll invite Penny and Shay, and not just because Max has a mad crush on her. It will be all the submissives who love you best. I'm going to leave before your den of depravity corrupts me." She rested her hand on his cheek and gave him a soft smile.

"Thank you, Day."

She winked, and walked away, hips swinging so his eyes immediately dropped to the curve of her ass. It was a great ass.

Staff was beginning to trickle in. The look of surprise on Kellan Brandt's face at seeing him here when he was supposed to be away said a lot. "Still yours tonight." He lifted his glass. "I'm off the clock."

"Hope you paid for that booze." Kellan narrowed his eyes as he studied him. "You okay, boss?"

"Not in the slightest." But maybe he would be. Pulling out his phone, he stared at it a moment before taking his glass and going into his office. The phone rang twice and the saddest hello greeted him. Fuck. Rubbing a hand over his chest. "Hey, sweetheart," he said softly. "I need to talk to you." Her sob ripped his heart out of his chest and plopped it on his desk.

"I need to talk to you too. I'm sorry. I wasn't...I didn't...I'm sorry."

"Shh. I've been drinking, otherwise I'd be heading to the ferry to see you."

"I can. Can I come to you?"

He meant to say tomorrow was fine, but he suddenly wanted to see her now. The drive from Jensen's to Victoria had been hell. Without letting his mother know he was even there, he slept in her guest room and left before she was awake. "I'd like that."

"Okay," she sniffled. "Okay. Is tomorrow still happening? Even if we don't...am I still..."

"Yes, tomorrow is happening." He hadn't even thought of canceling her session lesson. Fuck, he needed to plan that. "Edge is always open to you, Claire, whenever you need it."

"Okay. Are you at the condo?"

"At the club. It has the best variety of booze."

She clucked her tongue. "Even I read the club's membership rules, Mr. Peters, no alcohol for those participating. It can get you barred from the premises. The owner's a bit of a hard ass, so I'd be careful. I'll see you soon."

"See you soon, sweetheart."

He hung up and tilted his chair back. Grabbing his phone, he made another call. One he needed to make.

Claire followed the bouncer through the club. In the pit, couples were beginning to set up while a few watchers were scattered on the couches. Her attention, though, was on the open door at the end of the curved walkway. More importantly, on the man leaning against the doorframe watching her approach.

She fought every inclination to run and throw herself at him. Uncertainty had plagued her the entire trip over. Even with the phone call and him calling her sweetheart, she wasn't entirely sure what her welcome would be.

The problem was she wasn't entirely sure *what* was going on with her. She hadn't enjoyed Jensen and his Lucifer, so why push it? It's like she couldn't stop sabotaging her relationships.

"Thanks, Davis," Oz said when she stopped before him. He looked tired and she felt bad about that. She was why he was on the road late the other night. Why he even wanted to talk to her, she didn't know. "I'm still not here."

"Right-o, boss."

"Come on in, Claire."

She stepped into his office and would've known immediately it was his. Something about the rich wood of his desk and shelves said Oz to her. "Sorry it took so long to get here. The first ferry was full."

"Claire, you never have to apologize for being here. Did you want a drink or anything?"

"A ginger ale would be nice, actually."

He smiled and lifted the phone. "You've been at Doyle's. Send in a ginger ale and a coffee. Thanks, Sam. Have a seat, sweetheart. And stop looking so anxious."

Rubbing her thighs, she sat on the couch and Oz joined her. Did he feel as awkward as she did? The knock on his door was quiet and a waitress came in with a tray of their drinks. She gave a small smile, and disappeared. Claire picked up her glass because she had no idea what else to do.

"I'm sor–"

"Don't," he interrupted her, his voice low. "Don't keep apologizing. Please."

"I need to, Oz. What I did was reckless and immature. I want you to know I trust you." She rubbed her thumb on the side of the glass. "A lot. What I feel inside for you is overwhelming at times. I loved Doyle but it was hard to love him. I always wondered why he was with me. I was this ordinary girl and he was about to become *Doyle Kole*."

"You're not ordinary, Claire."

She smiled. In the Cyanide world, she was.

"Doyle never thought of you that way either."

"I know." Oz's eyebrow arched up skeptically at that and she nodded, before repeating, "I know. Sometimes I hated him. I hated that I wasn't as important as the music. It was always the next album, the next song, the next tour. There was always something that took him away from me. Even his addictions took him away." Hell they had nearly killed him. She never wanted to feel the terror of seeing someone she loved overdosing again. Ever. Again. "When he got clean, I thought it would be better, easier. It wasn't. It was harder because he was still not mine. He would never be completely mine and he was everything," she finished quietly. "For a while. That night at Edge, I wanted to not feel so alone." Rubbing her chest, she watched Oz lean forward, his elbows on his knees as he stared at her. "Only I was. I was so alone. More alone than I'd ever felt before. So, I used something I found joy in and used it to punish myself. With Jensen–"

Lifting her glass, she took a sip, watching the golden liquid splash because her hand was shaking. Oz took it from her and set it down. "I don't want pain. It's not the sub I am. Not like that. Where it's not," Jesus. Say it. *Say it.* "You," she whispered. "I trust you, Oscar Peters. You need to know that. Not just with keeping my body safe, or my well-being, but me." She rubbed her hand over her heart and his lips twitched up in a small smile.

"Claire, I need you safe. I need to tell you about Olivia."

She didn't know who Olivia was, but apparently, she was on his mind. "Okay."

"Do you know why I created Edge?"

"I assume it wasn't to find all the single kinky ladies?"

"No. I wanted to provide – scratch that. I needed

to provide a safe place for people like us to indulge our needs. A place where a submissive who didn't have anyone could safely meet a dom and partake in a scene under supervision. I wanted doms to have a safe place to learn about what lived inside them, whether it was just tying up someone or something far more sadistic. It became my mission to create a safe haven. Did you know Doyle was an early investor for me? A lot of his money funded Edge, especially at the beginning. It was a beautiful day when I was able to pay him back, though he bitched about it. I had money, but nothing like was needed for the club. I needed to buy the building, zoning, construction, equipment, licenses. Fuck, I pissed out money those first few years. Even before that night he called me for help with that submissive, I knew I wanted to build Edge."

He picked up one of her hands and flattened it between his. Was he looking at the size difference like she was? "Why did you need a safe haven?"

"I found BDSM by accident. Or not. I had an asshole roommate whose father was kinky. To humiliate people, he'd abandon them at one of the sex parties that happened. A girl and I were the victims of this."

Claire figured this was Olivia but she said nothing.

"I was really young and everything I saw was arousing, scary and I wanted it. Badly. She…Olivia did too. She was a quiet girl, sweet, adorable in that awkward way shy girls are. The dad became my mentor and Olivia my submissive. Only we were both new. So new. And young. So young." He sighed when he wrapped his arms around her, and she held onto his forearms. His body was tense against hers.

"We don't have to talk about this right now, Oz."

"We do. You deserve to know. I worried about everything. From ropes to impact toys to aftercare. I was too new for her. She was too new for me too, to be fair. She wanted to dive right into it after a few weeks of what we'd jokingly called BDSM 101. I was not as quick."

He wouldn't be. He was a patient man. Three weeks for her body to heal, even though the last of the bruises had faded last week. As if he had known they both needed that extra week to arrive on the same page. "Why would you be? You were responsible for not just her pleasure but her safety. That's scary. I can't imagine being a domme knowing someone's life was in my hands. Jensen has a cage, Oz. A cage. You came over when I was on the cross because you knew I was feeling anxious. You being there, right there, made me feel safe and not just because you trusted Jensen to not hurt me, but because you were with me."

He lowered his mouth to her shoulder and whispered her name. "Remember, she was new and knew none of this."

She should've. The reason why Claire had gone to that munch where she met Doyle was because she hadn't known anything beyond her own fantasies. "What happened?"

"She slept with my mentor and his wife one weekend when I went home to see my sister."

Claire turned to face him. He lowered his head to the couched and watched her through lower lashes. Straddling his lap, she cupped his face and looked into his eyes. "How can you be with me when your first sub cheated on you?"

"Different times, different subs, different me. It

doesn't matter, Claire."

She nodded. "Yes, it does. It will creep in at the worst time. Maybe we get in a fight and all you'll think is that I'm just like her."

"You are *not* like her. We've discussed this already. If this isn't working for you, you tell me. Would you ever do that to someone again?"

She shook her head. "No."

"If time swung back and you had the choice, would you sleep with him again?"

"I like to think I wouldn't." But she had been so desperate, she couldn't answer that. Would she be able to woman up and tell Doyle that they were broken? She wasn't sure. She smoothed her hand down the front of Oz's chest simply to touch him. She wasn't that person anymore, even though it had only been two years ago.

What if this started to break and one day it was broken? Would she repeat what she had done now? "I couldn't do it again. Not to you, not to anyone. Not just because it would hurt you, but it hurt something in me. It took me a while to look myself in the mirror. Look how long it took me to seriously talk to Doyle about it."

"If life had been different for Olivia and I had asked her that question, she'd probably still sleep with them. She didn't see it as doing something wrong. It was something that happened. But in the end, who knows. We'll never know because she died."

Claire met his gaze and saw the sadness in the greenish brown eyes. "Oh, Oz."

"I broke it off with her because she broke my heart and a month later, she was dead. She died on a St. Andrew's cross and nobody knew she was there. Her desperation for what was inside her drove her to a bad deci-sion. She died and a boy's life was irrevocably changed, along with his family's."

"And you. You were changed too."

He nodded slowly and she wrapped her arms around him. His arms banded behind her in a fierce hug. She couldn't imagine what that had done to him. "It wasn't your fault, Oz."

Bringing up Olivia had left him feeling a little mel-ancholy. What a tragic waste.

What he discovered was that she had returned to Brock and Kerry, hoping for more scenes. Unfortunately, once Brock had gotten what he wanted, they left her adrift. From Dayna, he learned that in that small group, Olivia's reputation had taken a hit. Desperation had landed her in the inexperienced hands of Joshua Avery.

They went to his dad's place to use the equipment and things had gone horribly, horribly wrong and Ol-ivia had died from asphyxiation. All his old roommate knew was that Olivia liked it kinky and she hadn't known enough on how to make the situation safe for herself or even Josh. In his panic, he left Olivia's body tied to the St. Andrew's cross. It had been a horrific discovery for Brock and Kerry to discover when they came home from their vacation in Mexico.

Oz hadn't gone to the trial. Her death may have been accidental, but Josh had left her there. After the trial, Brock and Kerry moved. They divorced a few months later and Josh never finished university since he had been in prison.

If he had been forgiving or taken her calls the first

few days after their break-up, how different would every-one's lives have been?

Olivia was why there was Edge so no one made the desperate decision to scene with someone inexperienced.

"Are you okay?"

He glanced at Claire. "Just thinking thoughts that make me not good for company." Another whose desperation had driven her to do a scene that went horribly wrong. The parallels made him feel a little nauseous. His mind easily replaced Olivia with Claire. Fuck.

"You just told me about your first submissive who died on a cross, after seeing me on a cross upset you. It's okay to not be okay."

Christ, she was such a sweetheart.

She leaned against him, gazing up at him. "The last time I was here, you told me to write an essay about the difference between you simply topping me or caring about me. I didn't, but I've been thinking about it a lot, especially as Thursday approaches. Jensen's was the difference. You stood there *with* me when I was on a cross because you knew I needed to answer a question. You allowed me to explore and learn. Considering your past, I'm frankly surprised you took a chance on me at all after that night at the club. You keep using the word desperation. She was desperate to ease the craving within her. Like a junkie. I did the same thing. I was so desperate to reconnect with who I was before the divorce. I missed being submissive. I missed it because I blocked it off. I was so terrified to find someone who wasn't Doyle. I messed up. I know that. Even had we never progressed further than you shutting down my mistake, I knew I was in a bad headspace. I promise that I will never do that again.

I know it could've ended way worse than it did. If I was a different kind of sub, it would've been a catastrophe. I'm not her, Oscar. I'm really not."

"I know," he said as he ran his hands down her back.

"I'm well aware that I could've been. For that, I'm truly sorry. To you, to that dom, for everyone who witnessed it, to Doyle and even my girls."

"I know you're not her, but I'm not Doyle either, Claire."

"Definitely. You're way more diabolical than him. You're all about the long game. Three damn weeks, Oscar," she whispered. "Three."

If he was being honest, he'd tell her that if he knew she'd wind up being here with him, he might not have put the three-week abstinence on her. Although, no, he probably would.

"Some lessons need to be absorbed."

She made a huffing sound that puffed out her lips. "No kidding."

"Will you come home with me, Claire?"

Her smile was enchanting. "Absolutely."

April 1989 – Oz

This wasn't how it was supposed to be.

There was this empty place inside him where she lived: a place full of music and love. Ever since he received The Call from his mom, that Kelsey shaped spot had been quiet. Jesus, he missed her.

A hand squeezed his shoulder and another "sorry for your loss" was spoken by someone, anyone. He didn't look. He didn't care. It *was* a loss. Did anyone realize just how much of a loss it was? Did they fully comprehend that he'd never receive another recording from her? That her piano would never be touched again? That the music she played was forever silenced?

"You should eat something," Dayna said quietly, sitting beside him.

Her presence at Kelsey's memorial had been an unexpected welcome. She had walked in with Jamie and Penny and his first thought was relief in that he wouldn't be alone. "I'm okay," he told her, squeezing the hand she set on his thigh.

"No, you're not."

No, he wasn't.

The Call changed everything and ended something. Kelsey had never truly been the same after her suicide attempt, her light a little dimmer and her joy in music diminished. None of them knew how to reignite the passion in her. His father's solution was to leave while Oz and his mother tried to show her there was more beyond her music room.

For Kelsey, there hadn't been more. Music was her world, her language and when it turned on her, she was lost. Until one day his mom phoned, crying. She was playing the piano again and it was beautiful.

It wouldn't last. The piece that eluded her, tortured her, was finally conquered. Mom said it was breathtaking, the best Kelsey ever played. Her mountain climbed. And once she was at the peak, his beautiful sister…let go.

The Call, now forever capitalized in his life, came shortly after. His fairy princess sister was gone. The anxiety and depression that had clung to her since December had beaten her down, the music she played a good-bye to their mom and to him. Her last recording to him was still in the padded envelope that had been addressed and waiting at the front door to be mailed out.

"You're a friend of Oscar?" His mother's voice was shaky behind him but she was holding on. The memorial was truly for her, a way to share her daughter with those who had never truly understood her. A quartet played Mozart in the corner, soft enough that everyone felt the beauty of the music but not loud enough to intrude.

"I am," he heard Jamie say. "I'm sorry for your loss, Mrs. Peters. Kelsey was an original spirit in the world."

"You knew her?" She sounded so surprised.

"I did. Oz brought her sailing. I own a boat that specializes in whale watches around the island."

Oz found himself smiling as he remembered that day. It had been a grey February day when he impulsively took his big sister for a day on Jamie's boat. Her laughter and delight in everything: the boat, the sailing, the dolphins and the whales, would remain with him forever.

"Oh," his mother said softly, surprised, as if she had forgotten Kelsey's stories.

"She said sailing was Tchaikovsky's Waltz of the Flowers, the dolphins were Ravel's String Quartet in F second movement and the whales breaching were Debussy's Clair du Lune. She sent me the three pieces she told me of and you know what? The next sail, I played her tape and she was right."

"She must've liked you, Mr..."

"Hennessy. But call me Jamie. And why do you say that?"

Did Jamie know the gift he just gave his mother? Oz didn't think so. "She only sent recordings of her playing to people she liked."

"That was her? Then I am doubly honored. One day when this isn't heavy on your heart, you come take a sail with me and you can listen to what your daughter saw."

His mom sniffled. "I'd like that, Jamie. I'd like that a lot. Excuse me. I can't stop crying."

"Go on, dear," he said, "a girl like that deserves to be remembered in tears."

Oz looked over his shoulder to see the sadist hold his mother tenderly as she wept all over him. Penny, his submissive, laid her hand on Jamie's back, then joined them. She too was crying and she rested her head on Oz's shoulder. "My heart hurts for you and your mother," she said. "I liked Kelsey."

He smiled for the first time that day. "Thank you."

"For what? Crying on you?"

"Yes." He loved that his friends met Kelsey. That these kinky, slightly twisted people had not just met her but understood her in way few did. He kept an eye on his mother, who dried her eyes with the handkerchief Jamie had on him. She gave Oz a watery smile and mouthed "I love you," to him.

"I love you too," he told her silently. Kelsey gave them that back in December. That, he realized, was her true gift. They weren't strangers who just happened to be related. Trauma brought them closer, pain united them. They lost their Kelsey, but her love? He felt it every day.

Chapter 16

FOR THE FIRST time, entering his condo didn't fill her with nerves, just a sense of awareness. He didn't turn on the lights, just held her hand as he led the way to his bedroom.

Her heart began to race and her stomach felt jittery when he flicked on the bedside lamp. As he started to draw her shirt up, she clamped her hands down on her stomach, halting the movement. "You said Thursday." Wait. What? His gaze studied her, his fingers brushing over the bared skin. The fluttering in her stomach took wing.

"It's midnight somewhere."

"You said Thursday," she repeated in a softer voice.

"You say that like you want me to stick with it."

Claire nodded, surprise moving through her. "I don't want you to compromise your demands. Yes, I'll beg and probably whine about them, but they're important to you. To me. Compromise elsewhere but not in–" she waved her hand as she searched for the right word. "Not as my dom." Yes, that.

His fingers trailed down and he released the fly of her jeans. "You've surprised me. Midnight is in," he looked at his watch, "three hours."

"Thursday," she repeated quietly.

"It means that much to you?"

She nodded and he sank down, dragging her jeans and panties down. At her feet, he slipped her heels off, glancing up at her. She shrugged a shoulder. Yes, she had dusted off her high heels for him. Bracing her hands on his shoulders, she lifted one foot then the other for him to undress her.

"I think I can pass three hours," he said, caressing his hands up her legs. He caught her hips and spun her to face the bed fast. When his hands slid up her stomach, she arched into the heat of his palms. She sighed when he cupped her breasts, squeezing them until her nipples swelled in anticipation. "Arms," he murmured against her ear and she lifted her arms up so he could remove the lightweight sweater. "Leave them up."

Her eyes closed, his fingers trailing lightly down her arms and under the lace cups of her bra. He peeled the fabric down so they were snug under her breasts, his hands caressing down to her stomach. A hand slid to her back and he gave a hard push that bent her forward, her hands falling automatically to the bed.

"Don't move."

Holding her position, she wondered what he was getting. Considering her pose, she figured either an anal plug or a spanking.

Wait. Was that the shower?

Lifting her head, she glanced at the door to his en suite. What was going on? Still she stayed in position because for all she knew, he was running the water and standing in the doorway, waiting for her to move.

She lost track of time as she waited, but eventually he came back.

"Are you sure you want to wait until Thursday?"

Before she could answer, he cupped her hips and pressed his cock against her. He thrust teasingly against her until a moan slipped free and her body responded. He worked her along the length of him until the thick head rubbed against her clit. God, he felt so good against her. She could feel herself on him as he glided back and forth.

"Think I can make you come this way?"

She knew without a doubt he could. Her fingers curled into the bedding as he drew her into him so her ass brushed his stomach before he eased her away. A sharp crack of his hand on her ass made her cry out, her hips jerking.

"I asked a question and I expect an answer."

"Yes," she gasped out.

He gave a second hard spank that she felt shiver up her spine and down through her pussy. "Answer properly."

Oh. "Yes, Sir, you can make me come this way." Any way. Every way.

"I do like how wet you get when you remember your manners. You still want me to wait?"

"Yes, Sir."

He slid a hand around to her stomach and down to her pussy. "Positive?"

She nodded, unable to speak when he rubbed her clit while sliding against her.

"Okay." He grabbed her hips and pushed her onto the bed. "I was wondering what I could do to you for three hours before I realized the answer was simple. Anything. I can do anything I want. Let's start with filling all these holes of yours. They may not seem eager to be filled, but you never know. They could be lying."

He nudged her legs open and the mattress swallowed her cry when he pushed a dildo into her. No. Vibrator because it began to move inside of her and he manipulated the front ears to frame her clit. He slicked lube over her anus then shoved a dildo inside her.

He straddled her back, cupped a hand under her chin and lifted her head. "One more hole. Open up," he said before sliding a stubby phallus-shaped dildo into her mouth, muffling her moan. It was her dream, she realized. The one she'd described in the car ride to Jensen's. "One of these could be my cock but what my sub wants, my sub gets. Thursday it is."

An idiot. She was a total idiot.

"Hm. I'm forgetting something." He gave her ass a sharp pop of his hand. She heard a drawer open and humming, he searched for whatever he felt was missing. "Ah. Yes, these will do nicely." He returned and rolled her onto her back. Leaning over her, he licked her nipple until she was arching, her hips writhing from the vibrator. Oz slid what looked like a rubber tip on her nipple, squeezed, then released. She gasped as it pulled on her nipple. He decorated the other one. Her hands searched along the mattress. He grabbed one, stretched it over her head and wrapped some rope around her wrist. With both hands tied, she could only feel. She licked and sucked the gag, wishing it was him as she looked at the sexy naked man lounging beside her.

"You are so beautiful," he told her, brushing her hair

out of her eyes. "I don't tell you that a lot. When you submit, when you rock your exhausted baby, when you hold me through a shit storm of the past. You are beautiful." He slid the gag free and kissed her. She clutched the ropes because she couldn't touch him, her tongue meeting his. Oz lifted his head. "Now, let's see if you can scream." The dildo was pushed back into her mouth and he reached behind him. She prepared for a crop or a flogger. Instead, he held a small metal pinwheel. He waggled his eyebrows and drew the thin spikes over her breast, down her stomach and over her tortured clit. Over and over the vibrator and the wheel worked her clit until her orgasm crashed through her. "Not quite a scream. Let's try again." He popped off one cap on her nipple. As the blood surged back into the swollen, sensitive tip, her eyes rolled. The wheel felt like he was stabbing her nipple even though it didn't break the skin. Too much, too tender. Then came the second nipple being freed.

He got the scream he was looking for.

He went looking for more.

His ringing phone jerked Oz awake. Beside him Claire mumbled about not yet. Reaching over he grabbed the handset while rolling out of bed. Hitting the talk button, he walked out of his room. "This is Oscar."

"Are we still meeting at noon?"

Rubbing a hand over his eyebrow, Oz looked out the window to see it was morning. So much for ringing in 12:01 by being inside Claire. They had fallen asleep and that had been that. "Yeah. Why are you up so early?"

"Some asshole wanted to meet at noon," Jensen said. "I thought if I'm up he should get his lazy ass up and meet for pancakes."

"Noon."

"You say that like you're going back to bed. Just so you know, redial is a beautiful thing. And I know you'd never turn your ringer off. Who's going to win this, Peters? Who?"

Oz hung up and stretched, walking into his bedroom. Claire still sleeping. He gave her bum a swat and sat on the side of the bed. "I'm meeting Jensen for breakfast. Did you want to join us?"

"Do I have to?" Her voice was muffled by the pillow and sleep.

"No. I'll leave a key for you on the dresser. Can you meet me at the club at noon?"

"You said four."

"I'm changing plans."

She rolled over and stretched, her breasts soft and tempting. With her eyes heavy with sleep and her hair a mess, she was utterly beautiful. His gaze took in every inch of her naked in his bed. Reaching down, he feathered his thumb over a nipple until it too stretched awake. Oz leaned down and licked the tip, drawing it into his mouth. His hand disappeared under the sheets. Her legs parted and she arched with a sigh. His fingers slid over her pussy, enjoying the feel of her.

He flipped the sheet off her and sank down onto her. "It's Thursday," he told her, kissing her. Her fingers combed into his hair and he swallowed her cry as he thrust deep into her.

Jesus, it was like coming home.

As if on cue, the phone began to ring. Since it was Jensen being an ass, he'd let voicemail pick up.

Claire's legs hooked over his hips and she rose to greet his thrusts. He tangled his fingers in her hair, watching her face.

He could've been doing this for weeks. *Weeks.* But no, he just had to go and issue decrees and shit.

Lesson learned? Probably not.

She clutched his wrists, holding on as they came together. She made the sexiest sounds, whether it was a gasp of pleasure or hiss of pain. He wanted to learn every noise she made and what it meant. *Three weeks*, his dick told his brain. *We could've been inside her for three weeks, asshole.*

"Oscar?"

"Right here," he answered. *Right fucking here.* He thrust harder and deeper into her just to hear those gasping cries she made when she was about to come. He lowered his lips to her ear, her body arched and straining beneath his. "Come for me, Claire," he ordered softly.

She tightened around him, a final cry escaping as she hit her release. *Mine* he thought; he followed her, emptying into her. He shifted them so she lay on him, her body soft and relaxed over his.

After a few minutes, a sigh brushed over his throat. "Fine. I'll have breakfast with you."

Fuck, this woman. She was his and he was never letting go again.

She was surprisingly nervous as she knelt on the floor. Waiting for Oz was, for the first time, causing apprehension and she didn't know why. This wasn't her first scene ever, or even the first one with him. Was it the room? Was it because they were back in the club? Or was it because they weren't alone?

"Now that, my friend, is a pretty sight," Jensen said, his shoes appearing before her. The hiking boots had seen a few miles and the original brown color was almost obliterated from flecks of paint. "Whatever are you going to do with her?"

"I think we should make her work for orgasms." Oz combed his fingers through her hair, the gentle touch making her eyes close. Until his hand fisted and he yanked her head back hard enough to make her yelp. She gazed up at the man looking down at her. "Her orgasms are easily come."

"Nice pun," Jensen said, giving Oz a high-five. "Are we going to shove dildos up in her holes?" She wasn't entirely sure why they were at the club so early. Breakfast had been enjoyable, but now they were here, far earlier then Oz had originally told her.

"No. Let's make her scream."

"You have the best play dates."

Oz tugged on her hair. Releasing her, he walked to his bag on one of the couches and returned with the collar. If she had been wearing panties under the short, short, really short cheerleader skirt, they'd have been wet. Instead she shivered as she felt her body's response on bare skin. Her shirt was another crop top, the navy and white matching the skirt. The breasts were cut out and pom-poms were attached to clamps covering her nipples. The swollen tips throbbed as Oz walked back, swinging the collar back and forth, the D-ring hooked over his finger.

"I think you need color-coordinated collars for all your outfits. What do you think? A girl should have matching accessories." He laid the leather over her throat, crouched down behind her and slid the strap into the buckle. His finger slipped between her and the collar to make sure it wasn't too tight. "This outfit is adorable." He flicked one navy and white puff on her breast and she sucked in her breath when it pulled on her nipple. "Go team."

Slipping his finger in the ring again, he pulled on it until she was bent over her knees, her bare ass and wet pussy revealed to him. The collar easily slid along her neck and he caressed down her spine and under the couple of inches of fabric. Her palms flattened on the floor as he ran his finger over the seam of her ass before pushing into her pussy. Her legs parted and her hips lifted, all without a thought. As he worked his finger inside of her, tiny, needy sounds escaped. A second finger joined in and she squeezed around him, her body moving into his stroking fingers.

When a third finger invaded, she tried to dig her fingernails into the floor as it echoed her cries back to her. Oh God, the feel of him inside her. She was never truly prepared with how good he felt, how her body welcomed him like he had been inside her for years. When his rubbing fingers found her g-spot, her entire body flashed hot. A sharp, short gasp exploded from her. Her ass tilted more, her knees sliding on the floor to grant him more access.

She was going to come. She felt her orgasm hot in her womb, and every push of his fingers took her closer. Between her spread knees, his clothed ones pressed against her, the denim soft and warm. He did something with his fingers that made her scream, a slow rub along the inside of her as he drew a circle.

"I want to feel you come, sweetheart."

Oh, she wanted to feel herself come too. She was so wet she could hear each glide of his fingers as they fucked her. Her body was all about sensation as he did another one of those circle sweeps. It wasn't a comfortable feeling, but Jesus it made her pussy weep. The yarn decorations on her nipples tickled and pulled as she tried to take more of him. How with barely doing a thing to her had he turned into this needy creature?

She barely recognized the pitch of her raspy cries as he continued to work her. His fingers slid out to the very tip before he pushed forward with enough force to make her body jerk forward. Again. Then again.

Hands gripped her hips with enough force to make her whimper. "Give me an 'oh,'" Oz demanded and buried himself inside her.

Her body shattered. Her pussy clamped tight and he jerked her back as deep inside her she felt him release.

"Oh," she whispered, tears spilling free. He was inside her. Not just touching her. Her pussy tightened around the cock that laid claim to every inch of her. Her fingers flexed as they stayed in the intimate position. Her submissively on her knees, body wide open for him.

Claire had no idea how long they remained like that, her heart rate finally easing. When he slid free, she squeezed to keep him there. He pulled gently on the collar until she was on her knees. She could felt his cum mixed with hers trickle free as she sagged against his chest.

"What was that for?" As first words after being intimate with him went they sucked.

"I'm about to co-top you with another dom. I need both of us to know who you belong to."

She knew. She was pretty sure his name was written on her soul.

Without any warning, he reached down and released both the clamps on her nipples. The fire that followed when blood returned made her shriek in pain and flatten her hands over the offended areas.

"Well," a voice drawled the couch, "that sounded promising." When she looked at Jensen, it was to see him lowering a camera.

"Yes," Oz drawled, easing away from her. "Yes, it did." A hand on her shoulder told her to remain kneeling, and he rose up behind her. He wandered back to his bag, searching for something. When he returned, her attention was locked on his hand holding coiled leather.

If Oz uncoiled a whip, she was safe wording her way right out of the building. While she confessed to being intrigued by *some* of what Jensen did, a bullwhip was not on that list. At all. She readied the word sunshine when Oz flexed open his fingers. A whip didn't slither open. Was that – she blinked not quite sure of what she was seeing. Was that a dog leash? She stared at the looped handle on the floor, still gawking as her dom reached down and clipped the clasp to her collar.

Yes. Yes, it was.

No one would ever think this was sexy or right. The thin black leather slid between Oz's fingers until he held the handle. When he crouched in front of her, she shifted her gaze to him.

"We're going to have some fun with you, Claire. Nothing used will leave a lasting mark as I want all this pale, redhead skin nice and ivory for your session lesson tonight. Think of this as a warm-up session on what is to come. I fully planned to implement the lesson, but I've decided that it will be Jensen. Between you pushing yourself and a dom to the breaking point and talking about Olivia, I think a session that takes a submissive to the point where they use their safe word is necessary. I want everyone to see the dangers of playing in deeper waters. That being said, I want you comfortable having Jensen scene with you, hence him participating. If you say sunshine, we'll stop and re-evaluate. We can either continue or the scene will end. Okay?"

She nodded.

"I'm digging the top, sweetheart," Oz said just before he flicked his wrist and snapped the leather handle across one bared breast. She yelped at the pain even as her body responded. A tug on the leash and he began to walk her through the club.

The floor, she realized, was interesting. Not a flooring she was familiar with as it wasn't hard on the knees. It felt rubbery.

As Claire crawled where Oz led, she finally understood why other submissives did this: the collar, the leash, the subjugation of crawling. The stairs down into the pit were iffy, but she managed it, feeling a sense of pride.

She felt *owned*. Not like a possession or a thing, but owned in the way that she belonged with him…to him. One thing Doyle told her about BDSM was that it was all about trust: you trusted the other person with all the filthy secrets and desires you even hid from yourself. It was a trust that was unparalleled.

Oz would never belittle her because crawling or kneeling fulfilled her needs in a way a hug never would. Others in the community wouldn't trivialize her fun and frivolous costumes because they brought her joy and everyone had a little kink to their kink that brought them joy. Crawling across the floor, wearing a collar and a slutty cheerleader costume wasn't something to be mocked, it was to be celebrated.

And in that feeling of ownership Oz gave her, he celebrated all the little pieces of her.

If he wanted her crawl tonight at the club, she would. Not because he demanded it, but because it satisfied a little kink to his kink.

She missed this. She had forgotten what submission was at the core of it. It was weird and beautiful and sexy and fun and filthy.

That made her think of the dom from that night and she winced as Oz gave a little tug on the collar. She *had* mocked fulfilling his needs. And hers. Plus, he had been punished for her selfishness. Thinking of that made her feel small and petty.

"Where's your head at, sweetheart?"

She gave a little shake of her head. It wasn't anything concerning. "Thoughts," she answered, simplifying everything.

"I guess we need to turn off those thoughts so your head is exactly where I want it."

Claire gazed at the spanking bench in front of her. Her stomach tightened at memories of the last time she was on it. Oz set his hand on her head and she looked down at her knees instead of the bench.

Jensen came over, caught the ring and drew it to the front. He adjusted the leash so it hung down between her naked breasts and parted knees. He adjusted the handle of the leash, then stood up. A soft click had her looking up and Jensen lowered his camera. He snapped his fingers and pointed down, telling she wasn't allowed to be looking anywhere else.

"I think you need to cut titty holes in all her sweaters, Oz. Those are some pretty tits that just want to be pinched, squeezed and spanked."

She had a sudden vision of pulling a top out of the closet and seeing two holes in the front. Instead of answering, Oz gave the leather a hard smack. "You're being benched, Kolemann."

She groaned at that one even as she sat on the leather which was cool against her bare bum. He pushed her legs open and sank to his knees. Oz's hands clamped firmly on her thighs and she watched as his face disappeared under the short flare of her skirt. The first flick of his tongue over her clit had her crying out and arching.

Jensen gripped her upper arms, holding her against his body while Oz's mouth did amazing things to her pussy. His tongue dipped in, licking away every response he drew from her. Padded leather cuffs were wrapped around her wrists, which Jensen clipped behind her back, preventing her from touching Oz. When strong fingers squeezed her breasts, shaping them, she gasped, cream spilling from her body to Oz's tongue.

Her nipples were pinched hard enough to make her see stars and her hips tried to rise to meet the dips and retreats of Oz's tongue. The two were so at odds: Jensen almost vicious in how he treated her nipples that swelled for him and Oz's mouth the sweet pleasure to the pain.

The two sensations swirled through her until she didn't know if she going or coming. Coming. Definitely coming. Her head pressed against Jensen's chest, her orgasm crashing through her. He unclipped her wrists and drew her sweater up, discarding it. Oz unzipped her skirt, lifted her hips and stripped it off.

She was turned and lowered to her back. They flipped her over so she lay face down on the bench, naked while her body hummed from her climax.

The bench was shorter than she remembered, her head hanging over one end and her ass nearly falling off the other. The two men worked together to set the lower rests in place before they clipped her wrists and ankles in place.

"She is going to pink up beautifully," Jensen said, running his hands down her back to her ass and back up. He gathered up her hair and pulled it into a ponytail where Oz tied it up with a piece of rope.

The sides of the narrow bench pressed into her tender breasts and she jumped when Oz's hand smacked down on her ass. "Yes, she is. Flogger?"

"Flogger."

Oh. Oh no, she thought as they went to retrieve their choice. She didn't need to see what they grabbed to imagine them. The heavy grip that held narrow strips of leather. There was a soft whistle followed by the bark of leather on skin. Fuuuuuck, she thought even though her mouth could only release a yelp as fire spread from her ass.

She had no idea who had struck first, but she thought it was probably Oz. She panted through the burn. A second strike with more bite hit her left thigh made her think it was Jensen. After that she had no idea who, there was only what. The strikes varied from hard, painful thuds to gentle brushes of the leather strips on her skin as if they were painting her with the strikes. Between that they touched her everywhere. She didn't know who touched her breasts, her back, her face, her pussy. Hands. So many hands with one goal: to arouse her.

One heavy strike landed on her ass and she swore she felt every strand of leather bite at her skin. Another then another. Just when she was ready to sob out her safe word, the hits ended. Her body throbbed and burned, her pussy shockingly slick.

"Remember Wallace's? And how we'd re-visit another fucking you?"

"Yes."

"Do you have an answer?"

"Yes," she whispered, craving whatever they would give her. "Yes," she repeated.

A gasp escaped when a hard cock slid easily into her, hands holding her hips. God, so good. Oz felt so good in her. She rocked into him, wishing he could go deeper.

"You bite me, girl, and you'll learn just how mean I can be."

She nodded once, and heard the grind of a zipper parting. Curiosity made her head lift as Jensen eased his swollen cock free, no underwear for him. Before she could process though, Oz thrust hard into her, distracting her. When her mouth parted to cry out, Jensen's penis slid in and muffled the sound.

Oh holy crap, there were two dicks in her. She moaned and was rewarded with a slow thrust along her tongue while Jensen grabbed her ponytail in a firm grip. She went wet at the taste of a man she barely knew who had just whipped her and was now fucking her mouth. "Damn," the sadist growled.

Her dom simply caressed his hands over her stinging ass, his hips pushing into her. She moaned, licked, and sucked, but mostly she was overwhelmed by both of them. The hand on her hair pulled her head back and the cock in her mouth slid free, allowing her to cry out each time Oz buried himself deep into her. She was dimly aware of her wrists being released but she still gripped the padded leather, needing to hold onto something.

Oz pulled her towards him and when the head of his cock hit her g-spot she saw stars. Every thrust dragged his name from deep inside her. She never wanted this to end and yet she did so they could start all over again.

He didn't tell her when to orgasm, she didn't need him to. The scene, she realized, came to the end the minute he slid inside of her. This was more than him topping and her submitting. Maybe it had been from the start.

She whispered his name as her body shattered. From behind her she heard him say "Claire" just as he found his release. The weight of him settled on her back, though he braced his hands on the lower bench with hers. The feel was comforting and sexy since he was still dressed. He kissed the back of her neck. After a few minutes, he eased up, lifting her free of the bench. Every muscle felt wonderfully relaxed.

"So that's the plan for tonight," Oz said, carrying her into his office. He sank onto the couch, holding her close. "I should get a bed in here."

Both plans sounded brilliant to her. "Hey," she said quietly. He glanced at her and she leaned in to kiss him softly. "I need to tell you something now because I'm pretty sure later I'm going to hate you."

He drew her into him, lowering his head to kiss her

long and deep. "I love you too, Claire. Stop procrastinating. This session lesson is happening no matter what you say."

"I hate you, Oscar. I really hate you."

Epilogue

July 2010

AS HONEYMOONS WENT, not that he had a lot of experience with them, Oz decided his was pretty good. He and Claire spent a debauched week on Jensen's sailboat, indulging in every image he told her when they first got together. He supposed they could've gone on a romantic honeymoon in Europe or Hawaii or wherever other couples went, but that wouldn't be them.

Jensen knew the best private spots where they could do depraved things with their submissives. Another couple had joined them, friends of Jensen's who were also into sadomasochism. It hadn't mattered that he and Claire were the tamer pair. Pain wasn't what the week was about. It was about indulgence.

He glanced over at Claire who had, naturally, nodded off on the four-hour drive from Jensen's to Victoria. The weird wonder hit him again, as it did constantly.

He was *married.*

After moving in with Claire a year ago, he had cut his hours down at the architecture firm. The commute wasn't easy, even with the boat he bought. He worked at the house and it gave him time with the girls. When he needed a shot of testosterone, he'd go next door to see Doyle. Right now, his friend was in Toronto recording a new album with some producer who was popular in the rock world. His mother was the one who offered to take the girls so they could honeymoon.

"We're here."

Claire stirred and stretched. She smiled at him, only to jump when hands banged on the window and Willow screamed excitedly. "Oh. Here!" She fumbled with her seatbelt before opening the door, catching both girls when they tumbled inside.

There was laughter, hugs and kisses, and a lot of chatter from the girls. He didn't know two little girls could talk so much at the same time. Oz climbed out and stretched out the kinks of the drive to watch his mother approach. She looked exhausted.

"Did you get us a present, Oz?" Willow grabbed his hand, yanking on it. He pulled on his forearm, making her laugh when her feet lifted. He scooped her up and looked into her bright blue eyes that were identical to her mom's.

"Why would I get you a present? Is it your birthday? Is it Christmas?"

"No! You're supposed to bring us a present when you go away."

"I am? I thought I got the present from you because I was away."

She gave him a narrowed glare that reminded him of her father. She cupped his face and gave him a kiss. "There! Well?"

"Let me say hello to my mom first."

"Grandma, Oz says hi!"

His eyebrows shot up and he looked at his mom. Her eyes glistened from tears but she looked delighted at being called Grandma. A lot had happened in a week. He lowered his stepdaughter down and told her there was a bag for her in the back seat. "Grandma, eh?" He wrapped his arm around his mom's shoulder. "How'd that happen?"

"I don't know."

"Dani, look!"

The four-year-old took the stuffed orca Oz had picked up at a gift shop by Jensen's. "Oooh. Mama look!"

Claire finally made it out of the car and hugged his mom. "I need the bathroom. Let's go, let's go!" She herded the girls into his mom's house and they followed at a slower pace.

"Oz, look, we made the piano pretty!"

They had. The grand piano was covered in crepe banners with a welcome home sign taped to it. When he had moved into Claire's, the piano had moved into his mom's. He hadn't been sure at the time, but she wanted it back. Claire said it was welcome in the house, but somehow this was the right place for it. A new home for it, free of the ghosts of his father's old house.

Before his father died, it had been locked in Kelsey's music room. His new wife hadn't wanted the piano; his mother hadn't been ready for it so Oz took it to his small condo. Now it was home. Willow climbed up on the bench seat and his mother lifted Danielle on it, who watched her sister with utter delight as if she was playing one of the masterpieces instead of plunking out a scale.

Claire came up behind him and wrapped her arms around him, kissing the back of his neck. "No, Willow. You made it beautiful."

A few more words...

I didn't set out to make Olivia a member of the Cree Nation. It sort of fell into play that way when I was trying to figure it out. I knew she went to university with Oz but I wasn't sure of her major until she said anthropology. Well why that? Then she told Oz it's because cultures, especially her own, intrigued her. I knew going into this story that Olivia played a pivotal role in why Oz built Edge. He wanted a safe place for kinksters to play. When I asked him why, I learned of the tragic story of his first sub who scened with someone who had no freaking idea what he was doing and she died from that irresponsibility.

And it crushed me because as I got to know Olivia, the more I liked her. I wanted to save her, but knew I couldn't because both Olivia and Kelsey defined Oz and that would play out in his relationship with Claire.

I didn't know Olivia was Cree until it came to her safeword. She picked nakinam, which means she or he stops. In my search for a word meaning stop, I discovered there were all kinds of usage of the stop and finding the right one for this use was difficult so I picked one of the easier definitions. If I've misused the word, I apologize.

That wasn't my intention.

There was also a lot of time traveling in this books: to 2009 and 1989. Can I just say how hard it is to locate 1989 information on the internet? Hairstyles, fashion… Yes I was a teen in the late 80s but 16 so what do I remember about that? Nothing and my high school yearbook was zero help except to tell me how bad my hair was. Throw in this book taking place in not one but two different cities and I was so screwed, until I sent out a few emails.

Thanks to Michael at University of British Columbia (UBC) for answering my questions about dorms and Jill at the Victoria Symphony who gave me the programing from November 1989 and making me super ecstatic that Beethoven was part of those nights, who we know made Kelsey think of Oz. How awesome is that coincidence? In regards to the dorm rooms, I have no idea if in 1989 there were two rooms with two beds or four rooms in the four bed dorm rooms so I made it up for how I needed it to be in my story. Sometimes you just need leeway to make something work.

I'd also like to thank Elizabeth Kelly for sharing her amazing readers with me. They beta read the hell out of this. Thank you.

And to my amazing editor, Alyssa Linn Palmer, thanks for making me look good.

Want more for your naughty to be read pile?

Scorpio Stings
Scoring Lacey
Sarah Mine

And on the deliciously naughty BDSM side
Domme for Cowboy

The Edge Series
Claimed Book 1
Tempt Book 2: a novella
Yield Book 3

Erotica
Her Surrender

Bio

Jenna's writing dreams truly began one summer on the air mattress of her childhood home. There she tackled her first romance: a truly wretched attempt at a medieval historical. Upon finishing the purple prose laden story of (in her own words) crap, Jenna decided that perhaps the historical genre wasn't for her and she promptly began to write in a contemporary setting. If only the journey had been easy. She tackled category romances (and in her own words) felt like they were crap. She didn't have the patience for romantic suspense. Really, she just wanted to get to writing the sex. (hint hint, Jenna) Her romantic comedies were so traumatic that she stopped writing until one day she got a phone call from a friend who said "We can totally write this." The genre was erotic romance and it was (in her own words) like coming home. Residing in Calgary, Alberta, Jenna happily writes the naughty romances that make her mother sooooo comfortable. (not)

www.jennahoward.com